The Fate of the Constellations

Dedicated to my mother
and all those that loved her.

Many thanks to Emily Anderson for your support in editing this book.

Front cover image by Shutterstock and Michelle Savioz.
Images by Michelle Savioz, Shutterstock, Pexels and Microsoft Software.

Resources used from websites are listed at the end.

First printing edition 2023.
Publisher: Amazon Kindle

ISBN: 9798372257023

For more information: https://www.learnbytutor.co.uk

Preface:

The Fate of the Constellations is a combination of my love of the Renaissance art world, animals, Roman mythology, black holes, and the stars. This is a huge range of subject matters; to me, it's only right that I include this content in my book. Art galleries are antidepressants for me, and books are magical realms of imagination. I never forget as an adolescent, the time I read the Magic Cottage by James Herbert, and within the story, parts of a painting come alive- gosh, this hit me like an asteroid and I stayed awake for the rest of the evening to finish the book.

I started writing this book in 2008 and my story began with the tale of animals. I left the book for years until I went on a women's retreat and one of the group's leaders informed me about badgers causing mayhem with flooding because they were digging near the canal for food. Again, I left the book for years and over the following decade, dipped in and out due to work and other commitments. Alongside the interludes, I paid many visits to the National Gallery in London, as well as the Uffizi, Academia and the Louvre

Museum, and other astounding art galleries. I imagined paintings coming to life, changing, and evolving, taking characters from key Renaissance paintings, and making up a story around them. A whole universe began to emerge, taking place over the course of a week.

I have created fictitious information based on discussions at retreat centres, dreams, and other experiences, although travelling to the Milky Way is not one of them, but one can wish.

Information on the history of the paintings, animals, and the Milky Way has been researched through the website resources and I am forever grateful for the time these authors have taken to present their facts. Throughout the story, I researched my subject matter and presented many facts about the various creatures, constellations, and stars in the Milky Way. I created poems and short songs from chapter 10 to illuminate the urgency of the Galaxy Travellers' danger as they await their outcome in the Milky Way. There are Supportive Resources at the end of this book e.g. the names and roles of the different characters and more.

May you enjoy this book, be inspired by astronomy and 15-16th century art, take care of our animal kingdom, and visit art galleries, particularly the National Gallery (Trafalgar Square, London).

Paintings appear to you and me as 2D,
and may seem like a canvas with paints on them,
but in fact,
they are your transportation to another realm.
Be attentive when you look,
for you also can get lost in the picture, and travel
beyond our world, to a magnificent empire.

CHAPTER 1

The Origin of the Milky Way

Tintoretto's Studio, Venice of Italy.

Monday 24th March 1575.

"I cannot believe how quickly I was able to complete this masterpiece. Titian will know who is dominating the art world now!" Tintoretto was completing his 'Origin of the Milky Way' painting, one of his masterpieces, he thought. This painter had chestnut brown eyes, silver, curly hair, and a long beard. Every time he was angry, he would use the tip of his paintbrush to comb his scruffy beard. Untangling his beard helped Tintoretto unwind and think more calmly. The Vatican commissioned a painting from Tintoretto earlier this year. The subject in the letter sent to him from the Vatican was titled "The Spirit of Our Galaxy." It stated:

"Dear Jacopo Tintoretto,

We are very pleased to inform you that we would like to commission a painting from you, for our church so that no one can touch it. You may be aware that the Medici family are ardent admirers of your work and art patrons. Their history and recent financial upheaval have brought the art world into jeopardy, therefore the concern of repossession of our masterpieces concerns us. 'The Spirit of the Galaxy' is the message that our beloved Pope received in his visions and this is the topic of our request."

Tintoretto deciphered from the letter that the papacy no longer wanted to share their paintings, or even worse, have the Medici take ownership of what belonged to the church's faith-goers. The seal of the church stamp was impressed on the envelope and the letter reassured Tintoretto that this document was legitimate.

Tintoretto had started painting the 'Nursing of Hercules' one year ago but he had kept it a secret. The masterpiece was based around the creation of the Milky Way which was inspired by a dream he had several years ago. Serendipitously, the papacy was requesting a painting based on the galaxy, which was exactly what the Nursing of the Hercules portrayed. The Vatican would never know that he had begun the painting last year and Tintoretto would claim that it only took him eight months to create this masterpiece. Little did he know what would unfold this evening and how it was going to take another six months to finish the painting.

When Tintoretto was painting the stars of the Milky Way, he would often think of divinity and the mysteries of life. The drawing had the feminine qualities of Juno and Ops who were resting on the bank surrounded by flowers. Although, many years later, this part of the painting would be detached, and the title 'Origin of the Milky Way' would replace its original title 'Nursing of Hercules'.

"Oh Tintoretto, you can never let go of a grudge! Titian said those things years ago and you must let it go!" said Isobel angrily. Isobel was Tintoretto's art technician. She was a slim twenty-five-year-old with blue eyes and auburn hair, which looked rose red in the sunshine.

"He nearly ruined my career, Isobel... How could I let it go?" said Tintoretto. To himself, he thought, 'She never listens to me and maybe she just wants to be paid, so instead of agreeing with me, she is forcing me to stop talking about Titian.'

"You always complain about other painters, but maybe, they also inspire you too, but you never THINK about that!" said Isobel annoyed at her master. Isobel had worked with her master for ten years, and he admired her audacity and clarity about things which would normally trouble him.

"Inspiration! These artists inspire me to drink more red wine than my hands allow me to. I want to be the greatest artist now! Titian has always been more popular than me. Time will tell," said Tintoretto as he began to remember that Titian used to be his teacher and that he should be more respectful in his opinions of his previous master.

As Isobel left for her home, Tintoretto moved the painting out of the crimson sunlight, into the shadow of his large art studio. As he blew out the candles and turned the locks of the studio, a curious noise came from the top floor. Tintoretto went upstairs to investigate the sound in the kitchen, but he saw nothing suspicious. He then moved back downstairs to his studio to do one last check. Tintoretto held his lantern which loomed on the oval staircase, growing larger as he walked downstairs. The gritted teeth of the iron bannisters made his shadow look like a circus performer who was falling from a tight rope. He unlocked the studio door, stepped one foot into the room, and saw nothing of concern. The lantern offered an eerie light into the workshop. As he locked the studio and front door, he wondered if his painting would be safe. Something did not feel right to him.

While Tintoretto left the building, he was unaware of the commotion beginning in his art studio. The Milky Way painting began to shake violently and the dark clouds inside the painting began to swirl at the speed of a grade-two tornado. The eagle holding the crab in the painting began to flap its wings and moved towards the silky bed sheets because it was trying to escape the strong whirlwind of the tornado. Juno the Goddess, and Hercules held onto Jupiter, who were all startled by the swirling clouds. All three tried to move away towards the distance and get to a safe place. Juno and Jupiter turned to see the tornado and saw the eagle was sucked into it. The eagle had lost its grip on the bed sheets and was being pulled into the vortex growing on the outside of the canvas. The bird's wings were flapping quickly to try and escape, but the wind was too strong. Then Juno saw the peacocks and crab were drawn into a dark hole that appeared beside the bed. Juno, Jupiter, and Hercules, along with four angels, flew towards the Milky Way, and they disappeared from the painting.

The tornado's wind speed grew stronger, and the eagle became separated from other parts of the painting and moved to the right of the drawing while the tornado joined the small cloud behind the bird which grew bigger in size. The black hole and the tornado were competing for energy, which made the painting shake even more violently. The blue sky turned pink and dark amber. Then, the eagle started to move towards the front of the painting and face the art studio. The eagle could see a dark tunnel in front of it. Its beak began to push against the canvas. Suddenly the area surrounding the beak began to join the vortex outside of the canvas, and a loud swishing sound, much louder than the tornado could be heard inside the studio. The circular vortex became bigger and engulfed the eagle. The eagle pushed through the tip of the canvas and became caught in the turbulence, unable to escape. The bird was swept through the storm and came out of the painting.

The frightened eagle flew around the studio for five minutes, before finding an escape through a gap in the large window, at the top of the window frame. The painting stopped shaking and became silent. It was restored to its original state with all the images but with one figure missing, the eagle.

Tuesday 25th March.

"What in God's name happened to the eagle?" shouted Tintoretto to his apprentice.

"I… I… I do not know. What do you say in Italy? It is missing a dark bird?" said Cristof very timidly. Cristof was Tintoretto's second art apprentice and was not particularly talented compared to Isobel. He was a young boy of 14 years, with brown hair, and green eyes, quite short initially, but seemed to have had a recent growth spurt.

"I know what happened: Titian heard about my masterpiece, and he came last night to destroy my painting! He is jealous that the Vatican commissioned a painting from me. But how did he know unless you told him!" he shouted angrily at the painting and Cristof.

"What?! That is impossible! I would never deceive you," said Cristof angrily without even thinking. Suddenly, he was aware that Tintoretto was looking at him in disgust, and Cristof's cheeks grew a dark shade of purple, like beetroot. 'How would it be possible for Titian to remove the eagle and repaint the background colours in one night?' thought Cristof.

Tintoretto stormed out of the room and walked upstairs to the kitchen to make himself coffee. He was so furious and felt that he would never be able to sell his painting to the Vatican because of the missing bird, which partly destroyed it. Tintoretto was losing hope of becoming world-famous before he died. 'What on earth happened to my beautiful eagle?' he asked himself.

Suddenly, Tintoretto remembered that he had heard something coming from upstairs in the kitchen last night, but when he went to check, there were no signs of a break-in. And if Titian did come to destroy his work, then he must have entered by the kitchen window and moved the upside-down chair to not fall over it. But the chair was still upside down and in the same position. The clumsy Cristof had to glue one of the legs back on after breaking it and had to stabilise the crooked chair on the cooking unit. The studio window was locked with a small gap so he could not have fitted through that. But even if he did enter through the kitchen, how did he manage to fill up the area with paint where the eagle holding the crab was painted? And how did Titian create the correct painting colours for the surrounding area, and to such a high standard, in so little time? Mastering the art of colour combination took years, but even the greatest artist could not put together identical colours in one night. Tintoretto always packed his art colours away, so Titian would have had to find the paint colours, and palette and have used something to combine the paints to achieve the correct colour. 'Or..' he wondered, 'did he bring his paints?'

Tintoretto went downstairs to his art studio and looked around for suspicious signs of entry or malpractice, but everything was in the exact place he had left it. He rubbed his forehead with his right hand, sat down in his large chair and placed his coffee on the side table next to him. He moved the chair directly in front of his painting and sat there for hours, unable to explain what had happened to the eagle from his painting.

Meanwhile, Cristof who had become genuinely concerned about Tintoretto, decided he would walk to Isobel's house and ask her to come to the art studio immediately. Isobel, alerted by Cristof and annoyed that on her day off had to check up on her master, stomped to the studio in ten minutes. She walked into Tintoretto's art studio, complaining that her day had been interrupted by him. She opened the door to the art room which Cristof had shut when he left to call for Isobel. Cristof was concerned that Tintoretto was going to do something crazy. Isobel shouted, "Tintoretto, what day is it to you?" She walked in front of him and saw his eyes glazed over. She could see the gold from Jupiter's milk, reflected in his eyes. She wondered if he had travelled to the Milky Way from his painting and would not come back to this world.

Titian's Last Journal, Venice Of Italy

Wednesday 28th March 1576.

‘This painting, the Rabbit of the Madonna! Ha! I drew it almost forty-six or is it forty-seven years ago!’, said Titian to himself as he began writing in his journal. ‘I lie here, ill. I cannot say that I will see the dawn of the new year, but I am confident that God will fly his angels to collect me as I ascend to heaven. The paintings I have drawn throughout my life were always dedicated to my faith. But that changed when I met the white rabbit.’

‘As I continue writing in my last journal, I am thinking about how Tintoretto accused me last year of drawing out the eagle from his painting. Ha! He is obsessed with the notion that I wanted to destroy his reputation. The fool could destroy his own reputation. I remember that strange afternoon when his apprentice Isobel knocked like a mad woman, on my home door. She was shouting accusations of many types toward me and I was keen to shut her down and end this show of stupidity. I let her into my home, and she was as red as the paintings of my Virgin Mary from my masterpieces.'

'Who would have known that my painting, the Madonna of the Rabbit, would have allowed me to travel to other realms of this world, by the white rabbit in my painting? I decided to draw the white rabbit again with the help of my technicians, that very day he disappeared from the canvas. I never told Isobel about my white rabbit which had disappeared the day before she came shouting accusations. My technicians looked at me strangely, that morning of March 1575. I never told them what had happened, and they were too afraid to ask. The white rabbit from my painting had disappeared but I never believed it was Tintoretto. He was my apprentice once, but he was not the type of person to damage someone else's work'.

'One month later, the missing white rabbit appeared to me in my home. The actual rabbit I had drawn on my canvas, came to life and was talking to me! Cosimo was his name: he explained everything. He showed me novel places of which I had never heard. Cosimo told me that he would take me to places that would inspire my art if I helped him to learn about the Milky Way. What great adventures I had on earth. What great magic we made on those canvasses. Long may my paintings last so people may enjoy them, forever.'

CHAPTER 2

The Rabbits Rabbitdom

The Red Maple Tree, Burlington, Canada.

Thursday Morning, 26th March 2020.

Rabbitdom is the name of the rabbit camp at Burlington. Each camp houses rabbits that have similar smells to each other. The Orchids rabbits all have a similar smell of eucalyptus and work in the Secondary Foundation where the atmosphere needs herbaceous freshness. The buckshots' and buckshells' enjoy amusing themselves with tales of the ancient folk and are sociable beings, so living in proximity is great for them as opposed to the badgers who are anti-social and live in smaller groups or alone.

The rabbits' lived under one of the oldest and largest maple trees in Burlington, Canada. The wood chippings from this tree were collected for their sweet aroma and warming qualities, which helped keep the new bunnies-kits (rabbit's offspring) warm through their first few months. The Burlington bunny camp spread for miles around them and housed thousands of rabbits. On rare occasions, the hard-working rabbits would leave to live in another bunny camp.

The durable maple wood smelled sweet and contained molecules that would help rabbits form long-lasting relationships with their loved ones. Male bucks called the 'buckshots', never understood why females loved the smell of the maple chippings, or what it did to their biology. When buckshots and buckshells (female rabbits) had offspring, the buckshots would bring buckshells extra maple wood, and this triggered the release of the love chemical oxytocin. The oxytocin bonded the rabbits with their offspring too.

Coco Sands married Little Bobbin the day he arrived at the Burlington community.

"I knew I loved you the second I saw your eyes," Coco said to Little Bobbin as they smiled wildly during their partnering ceremony.

Rabbits could choose a partner for life and live together in their private burrow. Little Bobbin had never considered partnering because he never imagined himself living with another rabbit in such proximity after having been held for several years as a captive, which expats called themselves. However, it did not take long for Little Bobbin to realise the love of his life was Coco. "You were my anchor here, and I will always be your partner to infinity and beyond the stars, my love. I love you more than maple syrup," said Little Bobbin in front of two hundred partnering guests, whom all giggled. The maple syrup flowed like magma that day and everyone erupted into states of joy.

In between dreaming, Little Bobbin hoped to see the elusive golden eagle because they were a good omen, and he needed it after his bizarre dream last night, reminding him of his captive home. The three children and all the other pets there made his previous abode a secure but irritating place. Little Bobbin loved humans, however, he found it difficult to spend time with them because he had to share them with different animals, 'They all stunk! I never liked the gerbils, they are so obnoxious and only think of food, and the meerkats just smelled bad, like earth rotting. Thank God that the silly meerkat called Mopster had created a huge burrow which led into a vast farmyard, and I met Thoric!' he told Coco and his friends when he first arrived at Rabbitdom.

Coco walked into her bedroom from the bathroom and saw Little Bobbin moving his paws quickly while he was dreaming. "Bobbin it is time to wake up, the robins are dropping maple syrup today."

"Oh, my goodness Coco, I dreamed of the Milky Way galaxy again and we were flying to escape some strange birds!"

"Oh my, your dreams are a bit wild. Did the birds steal the maple syrup?" laughed Coco.

"No, they didn't steal our syrup or wood, but I was with badgers, and we travelled to a red star in another galaxy," said Little Bobbin, oblivious to his wife's sarcastic question.

This humongous red star had red birds there that ate fish from lakes. The lakes were filled with flaming hot lava, and little fishes swam inside them. This world was vastly different from his. He still felt afraid as he recalled the details.

"There was something else too..." said Little Bobbin but he could not finish his sentence because there was a knock on their door.

"Hurry up and get outside!" demanded Coco. They knew that the knocking was from one of the friendly rabbits, alerting them about the maple syrup. 'My Bobbin has a fantastical imagination, but that is why I love him. Colour, how did he see colour?!' she asked herself. Coco did not have the chance to question Little Bobbin because he left swiftly.

Little Bobbin scurried through his home burrow still thinking about his dream. It reminded him of a time when he was a 'captive' and he would watch intelligent people talking inside a television box. The people in the box looked small and they never walked outside of the box. In one programme, astronauts were trying to find Artificial Intelligence within the Milky Way. So far, these people had created a spacecraft that could travel 50,000 light years without running out of solar power, but their space capsule would never make it to the Milky Way because it was 100,000 light years away. The astronauts still needed to work on their flying craft to make it more durable. Little Bobbin wondered if he would ever get to travel to the Milky Way.

But now, he saw one of his best friends, Captain Marlow. They hugged warmly and Captain Marlow said, "Didn't you hear the vibrations? The wood and syrup has been dropping all morning. Come on, let us grab some together."

They had bumped into each other on the nearest tunnel to the Queen Exit.

"Coco woke me up to tell me because I was having a deep dream about stars and strange worlds," replied Little Bobbin.

Captain Marlow knew all about his friend's vivid dreams and wild imagination. Like a scuttling crab, they sidled outside of the burrows and carried their crates with them to carry any collections. The boxes could hold five kilograms of wood chippings and syrup without breaking and would slide along the mud path to their homes. As Little Bobbin and Captain Marlow caught their first breath of fresh air, they could see rabbits for hundreds of yards around them doing the same thing. Gleefully, they wrapped four ounces of the syrup in some maple tree leaves to stop it from oozing everywhere.

The Monarchy

Rabbits held ranks of authority within their monarchy. Buckshots and buckshells were banded by their age, work abilities, and intelligence, but these rabbits did not have much of the latter. Rabbits aged 0-3 months were looked after by their parents in the Queen's nursery or the King's Quarter's groves within the Foundation Sector, deep in the earth. Then, from three months on, the rabbits moved on to the Secondary Foundation in the main camp. These rabbits were deciding where to go next in their careers. The rabbits also moved to this sector because they needed to get used to the cooler, damper atmosphere of their village. Many buckshell kits were sent to the Queen's Nursery where only doe's (buckshells) were allowed. Anyone above six months was expected to start taking shifts from 7 am – 7 pm, or 7 pm – 7 am. The best shifts were at night because the little un's would naughtily leave their camp and go furrowing out in the meadows, hoping to catch sight of the rare golden eagle or to see what life held outside of camp. The elder rabbits organised the camps and made decisions about Rabbitdom. The King and Queen of Rabbitdom lived separately and ruled the monarchy.

The Kerfuffle

Captain Marlow from the Orchid's family was on Brown Control, which meant that, since he was one of the eldest rabbits (ten years old) on duty, he had to make sure that all twenty apprentices were fed and rested, as well as check for incoming wood which was needed to fill holes or treat fungus problems. Brown control duties were based on the Secondary Foundation where the buckshells and buckshots had to work shifts. The Orchids were on duty from 7 pm - 7 am every day. There were always about five mature rabbits on duty, as well as Captain Marlow. Captain Lincoln or Captain Stripes would cover the shift when Captain Marlow was off duty. The comical rabbits enjoyed working and would spend much of their shift talking, creating silly jokes, and eating.

The captain had dropped his maple collections in his home when something overcame Captain Marlow, which saw him becoming quite strange.

Little Bobbin was returning from tidying up the maple wood outside when he saw his best friend jumping up and down on the Waterloo Bridge. At this time, no other high-ranking rabbit was around, and all twenty apprentices and the Orchid staff became very frightened, but they managed not to panic. They all ran up to the tertiary foundation where Laurel Tulipa worked, Little Bobbin's second-best friend.

Before the rabbits escaped to the Tertiary Foundation, each of them tried to get to safety by running along the bridge as fast as they could, just as Captain Marlow leapt upwards. Underneath the bridge was unadulterated, pure gold maple syrup. Of course, the rabbits knew they were taking a risk running along the bridge because who knew if the captain would take a small leap and then land on top of you! Once the young rabbits run safely across the bridge, they began to rub their noses with the nearest rabbit. This rubbing of noses indicated that they were calm. The rabbits did not want to be hit by Captain Marlow or cause him harm, but most importantly they did not want to show any disloyalty by running away, from their master. Rabbits were very loyal to their captain because, at the end of the day, no one knew who was related to whom.

Laurel shouted to the little rabbits, "good work my little friends, stay calm and walk to the end of this tunnel and wait for me there." As Little Bobbin looked closely, he could see water running out of Captain Marlow's left eye, and his scut (tail) turned from beige to black. 'Oh no, what has happened to my friend?' he thought. The black scut began to grow into a long tail, like a cat. Then his tail turned around into a coil. It is said that the robins high up in the maple tree could hear the captain yelp because all the birds flew out of their nests and returned two hours later.

Little Bobbin began tapping the earth with his hind legs because they were a lot stronger than the front. The vibration was extraordinarily strong and alerted other buckshots and buckshells in the foundation, secondary and tertiary foundations. The tertiary foundation captain would then tap their hind legs to alert all the other rabbits from the neighbouring foundations. It was like a fire drill that the rabbits practised every year on Hallow eve. The whole of Rabbitdom started marching to their allocated meeting points where their captains checked that the rabbits were safe.

The Queen and King's Council

King Roman and Queen Reina were eating a meal with their friends in their lounging room when they heard 'haaarrhhhhggg.' Everyone at that meeting recognised the voice of Captain Marlow. They felt a light vibration above their heads and in the walls alerting them to danger in one of the other communities. King Roman and Queen Reina sat straight up from their throne which had thin strips of maple leaves and French lavender buds. As they stood up the smell of lavender followed them. They looked to see if anyone was coming to their room. To the west tunnel, was the route to the Orchid community.

The Queen and King began to quickly think about their evacuation plans for Rabbitdom, and they were also very worried about their citizens. The royal couple were able to communicate telepathically, which led to their superior position on the Rabbitdom throne. Firstly, they were high breeds which meant that they would have had several dozen litters by the age of three, and their offspring always became superior ranks within the Rabbitdom community. They both came from distant lands. King Roman was named after his breed, the coniglionatura, thought to be from Italy. The rabbits were small and usually delivered a high number of kits. Also, their pheromones had an aroma that was of sunflowers. Queen Reina was from a Yorkshire family in England and came from a long lineage of royalty. They smelled like the sweet nectar of a mulberry tree.

CHAPTER 3

The Badgers

Ashdown Forest, The United Kingdom.

Thursday morning of the same day.

The badgers are the most advanced in animal communications. They worked out 60 thousand years ago that you could communicate with other badgers across the planet by travelling through the internal crust of the world. The clever badgers were able to create tunnels that could reach thousands of miles from England to Australia, from the South to the North Pole, and more. The tunnels were originally made of rail tracks with insulated wood cabins which the badgers had to manually control. The travel mechanisms used the heat of the inner core to propel the cabins. Recently, these transport contraptions were transformed into electrical cabins which featured a television screen, air conditioning and control options. The colonies prioritised installing a television screen so they could watch documentaries. Education was especially important for the badgers.

Most recently, in the last seven decades, the badgers flocked around nursing homes because the television would be on all day whilst they hid in the shadows. These inquisitive beings learned a great deal of knowledge from watching the telly: it helped that they could lip-read. The making of the inner channels to other parts of the world was a much-loved job because the badgers enjoyed the warmth from the fiery fires at the centre of the earth's crust. To overcome the mammoth heat, their hairs would create a protective sheet that allowed them to sweat and stay cool.

They would trade with others of the same kind, all around the world. There were meeting centres within the tunnels, much like a tube stop but with distinct types of shops.

The ingenious animals created Stop Centres where badgers worked and were reimbursed for food or tule which was the name of their currency. The Stop Centres had teams of badgers who ran the different centres. A few centres had map shops, others were trading shops, others were cub play centres, and some were workshop centres where they were taught skills to survive e.g. wood carving. There were over one hundred different centre themes, and in total, there are over four thousand different Stop Centres in the earth's crust. Twenty-two colonies had spent ten years creating a map of all the Stop Centres, which looked a lot like the London Tube Map. The different Stop Centres were shape coded e.g., Find My Friend Stop was represented as three spirals, and the Food Centres were shown as three triangles, and had a unique symbol to identify the name of the shop.

The English badgers loved Brazil nuts, so this is what they exchanged with the Brazilian badgers. The Brazilians thought the English cox apples were the sweetest on planet earth, and this is what they swapped their Brazil nuts for, but not all of them liked to swap! The British badgers learned to keep cox apples ripe by putting them inside the leaves of lemons.

Badgercom at Oakash

Oakash was the name of the badger community in Ashdown Forest. It was a magical community that had in recent years grown into a city due to the high number of them taking refuge there. There were badgers from various parts of the world, and it was brilliant because they learned a great deal from each other. It had a brown glowing glare at night, made so from the night fires in their homes. It was a happy city, a magical place that ran harmoniously, except for the rains. The recent weather of the last few months had left the badgers in a bad mood. The cold-averted animals hated too much rain because the outside soil would get sodden with water, and this meant they could not get close enough to the riverside to collect their food. The badgers enjoyed eating worms, roots, and fruits, which were their main source of food. Their large round bodies meant that they would get stuck in holes left by the rabbits, a nuisance if you asked any badger.

Boars (male badgers) and sows (female badgers) lived in their warm homes, low beneath oak, maple, and horse chestnut trees, and away from the noisy rabbits. Although badgers were contented living in the same shelters, they also loved their independence and would use their food-hunting time to be alone. The wintry weather meant that the colony had to find some way to relax within their homes, and what some of them found was that they could sit quietly with each other, unlike the rabbits!

Mulberry Cave

The boars had been discussing the need to hold a counsel meeting at the Mulberry Cave to talk about how they would search for food around the canals near Ashdown Spa Hotel, a women's retreat centre. The counsel consisted of a group of boars and sows that made decisions that affected the residents of Oakash. However, Oscar and Harper always made the final decision since they were the leaders of Badgercom. The community residents were too tired to travel to Stop Centres, and they did not have very much tule or apples to exchange food with the other badgers from other parts of the world. The sows were busy looking after their cubs and keeping them warm and fed, therefore they had been absent from the last few months of counsel meetings.

"Chilly morning, Bonobos!" said Winstone.

"I noticed, Winstone," said Bonobos, slightly annoyed that the first thing he started to talk about was the wintry weather.

“What has got you all cold, literally?” asked Winstone jokingly.

“I am hungry, how long will these rains continue? We need a plan with the counsel today!” said Bonobos, angry at the lack of counsel intervention over this serious matter.

“I am heading to the counsel chambers to ask for an urgent meeting, and we can meet for a snack after, Bonobos. It has been a busy day for me too so I am quite ready to do anything to eat tonight.”

As Winstone left Bonobos in his chambers, Bonobos wondered if he had been too angry and should not have shouted at Winstone. Bonobos was much older than the other badgers and had brought the city to its current utopia. His great, great, great, grandmother founded the city and named it after the largest oak tree in England and used the word ‘ash’ from Ashdown Forest to form Oakash.

The Round Gathering Of The Small Counsel

Winstone had been up since 6 am because he had been treasure-hunting by the river. Winstone loved to hunt human beings' rubbish bins and find frozen food so he could keep it for longer. He built an underground freezer using the rainwater running to the oak tree veins. He used the cold surface temperature to keep his food frozen by sitting them in ceramic bowls above the soil which was in his cellar.

Winstone loved watching television shows through the human windows and received an abundance of ideas from watching the Do It Yourself and gardening shows. This morning, Winstone discovered an old compass by the fruit undergrowth on the west side of the misty river. The dials were flicking very rapidly between north and south which confused him. A strange feeling took hold, there was something special about it and without further thought, he tucked it away in his backpack. Winstone loved antiques and had a cavern full of these treasures. If anyone wanted to see Winstone's treasures, they would need to book months in advance as he had a long queue of requests.

An Afternoon with the Boars

The badger named Llama returned to his home at 101 Oak Wood, Ashdown Forest. It was 9 degrees Celsius, so he began a log fire using pinecones. The oil from pinecones was useful for getting rid of fleas or nuisance insects. Honeycot taught Llama that the pinecones were great for starting a fire and helped to get rid of fleas. He loved Honeycot very much but had been too afraid to tell her how he felt. As he scratched some wood together and threw a piece of kindling on top, he heard a knock on the door and to his surprise, there was Honeycot. She quickly came in and sat on his oak chair which had been carved by Llama's own hands. This stunning chair was fashioned into a Buddha and sat by the fire, next to a small book table.

"What a wonderful surprise to see you, Honeycot," Llama smiled.

"I sensed you entering the city and I wanted to see you," Honeycot began. "I am wondering why you had arranged a counsel meeting at the Mulberry Cave this evening when it is freezing in the late evening. I know about your meeting because I just bumped into Winstone. He said he has been treasure hunting, felt very hungry and wanted to call a meeting. All the little ones talk about his treasure and get so excited about visiting his home. But anyway, I keep going off track, why are you having a meeting when it is freezing over?" she asked.

Llama sat down on his woollen blanket with his back against the wall and rubbed his paw three times against his nose. He looked up and his eyes were glistening due to seeing her in his home, but Honeycot thought he had a distant stare. He began explaining about the invites sent out earlier, "but I guess that only ten badgers will attend, including me. I hope to be elected as the Chair Leader."

"I hope Sparrowsky will be joining you, he is

a good decision-maker," Honeycot said. "You are the greatest leader of Oakash. I hold you in high opinion and I wanted you to know. So, continue..." she gulped, had she been too harsh? "Please continue, Llama," she said softly.

Llama had never heard her speak with such high regard for him. 'Had she always thought this way about me?' he wondered.

"Bonobos and I have concluded that to keep the city well-fed and improve everyone's moods, we need to take drastic action. Tonight, we badgers will drain some parts of the Oakash river so we can gather some berries. Well, to be honest, this is an idea that I have been pondering for a week, but I do not know what the counsel will think of it. My plan is for our brave badgers to create four or five burrows leading to the canal, which depends on how many attend; and then, as we get close to the water, we will dig a small hole for water to seep through. Then we will rush backwards and get ourselves safely out in time before the water pressure rises through the hole and creates a river trap for us. After the water subsides, we can walk back to the canal which would have dissipated, and then we will be able to reach the berries."

He looked into her eyes for a response and continued when he felt secure enough that he had not frightened her. “Bonobos will be meeting us too, so I feel confident that we will be successful.”

“But what happens if you get trapped by the water and you become stuck in the burrow and drown or catch hypothermia?” she said as she began to feel saddened by the prospect of losing him. In truth, she loved him, but she had not told him and kept her heart’s true feelings in a box.

“No. No. Do not worry, my dear. This will work, and we must take this drastic action for the survival of our colony. This city needs food and to do that we need to divert some of the water away from the Oakash river.” Llama responded. “Please do not worry about me, I have travelled far and wide, and I am strong, and you know how strong Sparrowsky and Agent Sol are, you were the referee at the judo match in the 2011 Olympiad games.” Agent Sol and Sparrowsky could be relied upon to attend this meeting.

“Ah great that you have extraordinarily strong counsel members, I feel a little bit less anxious now. Have you tried burrowing nearer to the Ashdown Spa Hotel, by the mud patches close to the large statue of the eagle?" asked Honeycot.

"Isabella tried it yesterday and said the muddy mess was caused by the rabbits, and there was no food there," replied Llama.

Honeycot's heart melted just as she was beginning to find a stronger connection with Llama. Regretting her outburst, she sat next to Llama and held his paws while she sang him a song to wish him protection and success.

An Evening with the Boars.

Bonobos held the meeting at 8 pm on the 26th of March 2020 at 5 Celsius and decided this meeting would last between 7-10 degrees Celsius and no less. Badgers measured time in temperature during the cold months. The counsel leaders always invited a minimum of two hundred and fifty badgers but only fifteen invites were sent today due to the urgency and time-sensitive issues. All important meetings were held at the Mulberry Cave and lasted no longer than two hours under these freezing conditions. You see, badgers had extraordinarily little patience for the cold and preferred to sniff for food outside their village than just talk.

On this evening, only eight counsellors came to the counsel meeting because of their hunger. Winstone was the second to arrive; he lit a fire to warm up the colossal cave, which could seat one thousand badgers. All around the cave were pictures of badgers who had won awards at their annual awards ceremony in Pakistan. The drawings were so spectacular and the fire smoke made it look like the pictures were moving. The other badgers all arrived and sat around the smell of the burning juniper wood. Winstone's fire was beginning to heat the large cave and the badgers began to settle into the meeting.

The counsellors had received letters through their letter boxes earlier in the day, requesting their attendance this evening, but not all invitees were expected to attend as badgers were generally lazy and moody during the cold temperatures. This malaise overcame most of them during the winter months because of the very few berries around, especially strawberries, as boars and sows loved this berry.

Winstone and Bonobos stood up and decided to scribe their plans on the dirt, "we shall write our plans here?" asked Bonobos, indicating the area next to their founders' tombstone. This was important because should anything happen to them, other badgers would know what the counsel's plan of action was and they would be able to find them quickly if the counsellors were missing for inconveniently too long. Winstone nodded 'yes'.

“Why are Harper and Oscar not here?” asked Sparrowsky.

“Hmm dear Sparrowsky, my dear old friend. I spoke to our leaders earlier and they said that Llama should be the leader of this group. They have taken refuge deep in the camp and have other counsellors with them to forge a winter plan for next year. In Oscar’s words: ‘I am tired of being tired’. He meant that he is so hungry, he feels under the weather and has no energy to go travelling,” Bonobos replied.

Decision One

Llama has been elected as chair speaker and leader at the counsel of Mulberry Cave by the counsel leaders. He will make the final decision tonight. We will call ourselves ‘The Oakash Water Diggers’.

Llama was over the moon that he had been appointed the leader and chair, and was looking forward to telling Honeycot. He was feeling tired lately because he had not eaten much food and he preferred to give away what little food rations he had, rather than eat it himself.

"I accept this duty," he said smiling through gritted teeth. He explained what plans he had concocted and went on to describe decision two.

Decision Two

We will create four burrows under the Ashdown canal to disperse the water away, therefore reducing the amount of water in the canal and creating an easy passage to our food source.

By creating water dispersals, the badgers would have a better opportunity to reach the berries and catch any worms which were good for the cubs. The water dispersal would run down the road and onto a farmer's patch of land. The water would not damage anyone's land and no human would be endangered by it.

The scribed plans explained that the tasks were to clear the water, along with a map of the location. The boars would use their strong paws to create a badger size hole from the bank to the river. Bonobos also wrote the warning symbol for 'drowning danger,' which consisted of water over paws.

Decision Three

We shall make the burrows straight after this meeting despite not receiving agreement from all the invitees of the counsel members. Each burrow will be made as soon as possible, which will fit two badgers per hole, two metres away from each other.

The badgers all agreed that they would create the burrows this evening because delaying any longer was not going to help anyone. To overcome the fear of drowning, Llama suggested they take turns burrowing side-by-side, and in pairs, and once they got near the water, they would just create a small lizard-size hole rather than a large-sized cavity, thus reducing the risk of becoming drowned. This small hole would eventually be filled by the canal water which would happen slowly, therefore giving the badgers time to escape from potentially drowning.

Decision 4

We shall be partnered like this: Figs with Tanto, Sparrowsky and Agent Sol, Winstone and Llama, and Santiago with Bonobos. Each one must carry a backpack.

Each badger will carry their backpacks with them for holding the food once they have access. The first two badgers Figs and Tanto would begin burrowing a tunnel ten meters away from the walking bridge. Sparrowsky and Agent Sol will burrow a tunnel to their right where there was more water pressure. They also run the biggest risk that water could drown them. Both Sparrowsky and Agent Sol were the strongest badgers in the group and had competed in the Olympiad's judo events in the past. Then Winstone and Llama will dig the third tunnel closest to the bridge because they are smarter than the second tunnel workers. Bonobos and Santiago will dig the tunnel furthest to the right.

This drastic itinerary has never been suggested, nor considered before. They run the risk of death. But the bellies of the colony at Oakash were beginning to rumble. Completely exhausted, Bonobos finished etching the plans and they all went into action. There was no time to waste.

CHAPTER 4

The Calamity at Rabbitdom

Back to Captain Marlow's scream.

Thursday Afternoon, 26th March.

Captain Marlow woke up from a nightmare, earlier that very day. In his dream, he saw hundreds of bucks' disappearing through a dark tunnel and humans were trying to clear the holes to save the rabbits. Maribel woke up as soon as she felt Captain Marlow sit up.
"What's wrong, my love?" said Maribel.

"A bad dream, that is all. Can you go back to sleep, or would you like a cup of camomile tea?" asked her husband.

"I am okay. Do you want to talk about your dream? It looked like you were having a nightmare," said Maribel, knowing that he would never talk about what bothered him. She had noticed this about him since the moment she met him at the annual Rabbitdom party.

"It was just a bad dream - of rabbits disappearing and..." he hesitated from speaking further and for the first time, she noticed that his voice was quivering. Maribel was surprised to hear the hesitation, and she did not want to make him feel too pressurised to speak, so she quickly changed the subject.

"Tomorrow, we start work on the new homes for the visitors and we have thirty rabbits from the Orchid's community coming to help make plans, so I am extremely excited. Oh, and we are getting help from Harlequinn and Patchy."

"I know my love; the little un's have been talking about the plans all day. Our beloved colony never stops improving our kingdom; their ambitions are contagious." Maribel went quiet and they lay back down and fell back to sleep.

The tail, and later that day.

Captain Marlow was gearing himself up for the day ahead after maple picking. He had just boiled a camomile tea and set it on the maple coffee table, when he started to feel ill. The captain had never felt unwell before but instantly became ill when his scut and whiskers began twitching uncontrollably. 'Perhaps I ate too much maple today!' he tried compensating his illogical thoughts for his uncomfortableness. The captain's insides started to make noises like the same sounds empty stomachs make when humans are hungry. Frantically, he quickly moved out of his room and headed towards Waterloo Bridge, but the smell of something so intense almost crippled the captain on the spot.

The captain began recalling the earlier kerfuffle more clearly: 'I must continue despite feeling disorientated and warn the rabbits,' he thought. So, he dragged his body with his front paws until he reached the bridge. He could feel his tail getting bigger and changing, which confused him because he wanted to move forward but his tail was pointing in all sorts of directions. He reached the centre of the bridge and started jumping up and down to make the vibrations, as a warning so that all the rabbits would flee. He jumped onto his hind feet to make his stomp as powerful as possible. Suddenly, he remembered last night's dream where hundreds of the rabbits had disappeared and he began to worry that his dream might come true. He instantly noticed dampness to the level adjacent to the bridge where he had jumped. He moved towards the dampness and an unidentified smell became increasingly intense as he approached the source. The smell reminded him of the big cat. 'Oh my God, the cat Luna has come back!' he thought to himself. By this time, the entire Orchids had moved to safety on the great meadows outside with Laurel.

The captain's scream was very loud and caused all the work to stop in their community. Several hundreds of rabbits, each with meticulous jobs, stopped their activity at once. This was the first time that a bunny could hear their whiskers bristle against one another, or was that down to fear and adrenaline?

The captain headed for the King and Queen's quarters when he unexpectedly met them on the passages for the exit of Oakash.

"My dearest Marlow, how are you feeling? The sweetness of our teas must hopefully bring you relief." King Roman said as he passed the captain a tea.

"The pride is fine. We think the big cat Luna has returned to haunt us again. Are you okay Captain?" asked the Queen.

"Yes, my King and Queen, I am fine now thanking you. I just received that sense too. I will climb to the outer burrow and start the clean-up job immediately. The awful odour of Luna's urine must be eliminated as soon as possible. I find the stench quite repulsive," said Captain Marlow.

"You are the wisest of our captains and we commend you for your jumping and scream," said Queen Reina. She meant this with all sincerity. Captain Marlow was the kindest and most loyal rabbit. He never rested until all the young un's had adjusted to their new burrows and knew what their purpose and responsibility were.

"My Queen, you are always the most gracious and kindest with your words. I can only thank you for your confidence in me," said Captain Marlow.

Soon afterwards, Captain Marlow went to the outer burrow, and he picked up the wet patch with his nose where the big cat had left his mess. 'What was Luna trying to say by urinating near our exit?' he asked himself. 'Was he warning us about taking all the maple chippings or did he sense something was going to happen?' Captain Marlow knew he needed to talk to Blazing Star. Blazing Star was the aid and main confidant of the royal couple and he trusted her intuition, and wisdom. Fortunately, there were thirty rabbits outside, including Blazing Star, who was clearing up the wet patch. Eight rabbits had brought water with them, whilst other rabbits had brought maple boxes to carry the urine-wet grass and mud away from the camp. The return of the big cat was worrying him, and he knew that talking to Blazing Star would help to clear his mind.

Blazing Star joined the clean-up team before the captain went outside, and she could tell that something was not right with her friend.

"You managed that situation well Captain Marlow," said Blazing Star.

Both sat down and drank warm lavender tea with its wonderful, calming effect. The rabbits would drink their tea and then sit in a circle, with their whiskers touching during their group meetings.

"Thank you for saying so. My scut grew larger, larger than any tail of any rabbit species, and my whiskers began to twitch uncontrollably," said the captain.

"Any of the captains would also react the same," responded Blazing Star.

"Maybe, Captain Maplelog is so composed. I have not seen him nor Captain Lincoln for weeks," said the Captain.

"Yes, it's been very quiet recently," Blazing Star said as she smiled out of the corner of her mouth. It was never 'very quiet' in Rabbitdom.

Captain Marlow knew she was joking. Instantly, he began to relax.

"Do you think Luna is trying to warn us about some dangers, Blazing Star?" asked the captain.

"Well, if Luna was warning us about an impending

danger, he sure did cause chaos today! The feline has a funny way of turning up when changes are about to take effect in Rabbitdom although whether these changes are positive are not, is not yet clear," she responded.

Captain Marlow took this in and breathed out the hot vapour of the lavender tea. They watched the busy rabbits work quickly to clear the urine mess from Luna. The captain and you, the reader, must remember that a minute in a rabbit's life is like twenty minutes for a human being because, in rabbit time, warp speed is exactly how they function.

"On another topic, Harlequinn is visiting our community to look at building another bridge. The King and Queen, as you know, want to build another level beneath the foundation sector. There is so much syrup around so another maple river would be amazing. Could you imagine if we fell into it?" laughed the captain.

Blazing Star knew all about the bridge plans and the Captain would normally be aware of this but he was off-kilter today. "No one would want to come out," laughed Blazing Star.

"Little Bobbin would love it. He was telling me about his dream this morning," said the captain.

"Oh, what did he dream about this time?" asked Blazing Star with a hint of sarcasm. Everyone knew Little Bobbin loved telling tales of his captive adventures and wild dreams, and his dreams were the wildest stories. Some rabbits would lift their front paws in the air as if to say, 'enough'. Rabbits were not always the most tolerable of unearthly dreams.

"He dreamt that he travelled to another galaxy, and saw strange birds which were red. The strange thing is, we cannot see in colour so how does he know that they are red, or any colour for that matter?" he asked.

"Sometimes, I wonder if Little Bobbin has travelled to another galaxy where all animals can see in colour. He is so adventurous, and I love his stories about being a captive and the meerkats," she replied.

"Me too," smiled Captain Marlow.

"All done up here now Captain," said one of the young apprentices.

Ten apprentices were carrying the box to a fire

pit that had been created by a Captain from the adjacent camp. 'This home of mine is great. I never want to leave here' thought the brave Captain.

Blazing Star

Blazing Star woke up at 6 am, as regular as clockwork, and went through the burrows towards the Lotus exit. After the morning had passed and by chance, she noticed the maple elevator had stopped functioning. She would need to report that later at the meeting. Blazing Star decided to ascend to the great green pastures outside and take a risk to eat early grass, on her own, which she had permission to do so. Going to the great outdoors was not permitted for the young un's in the Rabbitdom community and was instilled in the rabbit's mantra from an early age because of the threat of the cat or other large mammals like humans.

As Blazing Star emerged onto the land she felt a new freshness within her body, something which she had not felt for a while. Blazing Star inhaled very deeply and breathed out slowly, and then began eating the grass under the Oakash tree. As she did not eat as much as the others, her teeth would grow too large and cause her gums to feel sore. But after four minutes of eating this grass, she felt much better and the problems with her teeth began to vanish. The trees were beginning to wake up, and their leaves and buds began to grow. She saw squirrels jumping from one tall tree to another without fear and with fantastic agility.

After her nap, Blazing Star spent the rest of the daytime arranging plans with Harlequinn about creating a maple river in the lower sector of the rabbits' community. She was so excited and so were all the rabbits that knew of the plans. After her meeting ended, she was back in the factory domain working on the oak and sweet chestnut wood pieces and trying to glue distinct parts of the timber together. Everyone knew sweet chestnut trees had a sweet syrup that could make a good sticking adhesive, so she was trying to figure out which part of the wood was the strongest when she heard loud thumps.

King Roman and Queen Reina were calling her to a meeting. While she walked to the council chambers, the incredible idea that had brewed in

Blazing Star's mind since she met Little Bobbin two years ago at the meeting of the Waterloo Bridge, re-emerged. 'I must discuss with the royal King and Queen about the solar lights. I must, I must remember to discuss it today,' she thought. Little Bobbin spoke of this television program he saw which was from a box that had real people in it, although, he would say, 'I can never understand how so many people could fit into one box in one day, I always thought that people spent the day outside working on extracting maple from the saps'. This television showed people doing experiments with spacecraft and solar power. 'I got the idea of using solar power to light up our homes at night,' she told Little Bobbin. Blazing Star was extremely excited and wanted to tell the royal couple of their ideas. "It would make the night shift easier, especially when works begin on the lower foundation for the maple river. The rabbits would need light deeper in the earth," she told the Queen later that day.

Blazing Star stepped into the headquarters of the Queen and King and was greeted by the smell of camomile. "What news do you have for us Blazing Star?" asked the King.

"Let her sit down first before she begins," laughed Queen Reina.

"Pardon my King and Queen, we have had a busy day in the factory. We found a way to make the wood stronger and stick together in a cohesive way that the sap of the sweet chestnut and honey syrup will not break the wood," replied Blazing Star as she sat down.

One of the rabbits served her a drink of camomile tea with a teaspoon of honey, which was her favourite.

"Goodness me, that is good news," said King Roman.

"Harlequinn came to discuss the plans and all the operations involved," said Blazing Star. "She will be co-leading the project with Patchy too... the little un's are aware of our plans and news has spread like wildfire."

Just as Blazing Star was about to continue discussing her plan about installing the solar panels, a loud sound came from the underside sector.

"Haaarrhhhhggg," a voice shouted. It sounded like it came from a rabbister, a term the Rabbitdom community made up to identify someone who was older than ten years.

The elevator from the Orchid family which lowered to the Brown sector was out of order because the newly bred rabbit had accidentally dropped 20 pounds of the sweet liquid through the floor. Blazing Star's duty was to inform the King and Queen of any news and updates to the community but on this day, she was part of the news!

Blazing Star hoped that Captain Marlow was okay, she respected him more than any other buckshot.

The Buckshells' Strawberry Fields

Buckshells' kept strawberries frozen all year round in their secret undergrowth where they went to give birth to the cubs. The clever girls had learned how to grow the sweetest and fattest strawberries from the picture archives in the caves of Rabbitdom. The wall pictures showed images of buckshells growing strawberries in a greenhouse, which created the best fruit all year round and stayed preserved when stored with the juice of a lemon. A greenhouse was constructed of glass and kept humid temperatures inside, which helped grow the strawberries, even during the winter.

Laurel discovered that glass bottles could absorb sun rays and warm up anything underneath them. She also noticed that this object could create a fire so she had the idea that they could use the darker-coloured glass to create a greenhouse. It was safer because it created a shade that would minimise the risk of a fire.

Two years ago, Maribel and Laurel spent an entire day devising a plan to create a glasshouse. This action plan was called 'The Success to my Sweetest Strawberries'. They scribed their plan on the mud near where the buckshells gave birth, outside the nursery, where buckshots were not permitted to visit. Rabbits would draw pictures with instructions; they could not write as the badgers could. The rabbits observed the scribed plan that had clear instructions for their jobs.

Both buckshells' had to ask Queen Reina for permission to create the greenhouse and grow strawberries. Queen Reina was good friends with Maribel and trusted her hunch.

"I grant you permission as long as you promise to send me some of the delicious treats," grinned the Queen.

The project was kept a secret from the buckshots'. Maribel and Laurel recruited twenty buckshells to create the greenhouse using different coloured glass bottles, which they had over time, stored since the idea began. The construction work began by using the soil from the kitten's nursery where rabbits undergo kindling. The younger females stood guard around their camp, nose to attention. Nothing escaped their memories. They worked through the night and used the moonlight and stars as their source of light. The buckshells saw shooting stars, three days in a row on their first week of construction, which they thought was a very good sign.

Maribel and her best friend Twinkle decided before the building that they wanted to help with the more strenuous work by supporting the upright jars.

"You are both very strong than the rest of the group," shouted Patchy.

"We might need help at times so be ready to help Twinkle and me," said Maribel.

"We will be ready!" affirmed Patchy.

The rest of the buckshells' collected the glass jars and bottles and arranged them into a rectangular shape with the flatter glasses intended for the roof, and the other bottles fitting the walls. Any gaps would be filled with the shards either broken by the rabbits during transportation or found broken. The glass would be stuck together with the sap of maple syrup. The picture stories from their history wrote about the process of gluing using sweet nectar, and it was needed in those days to keep the heavy rains from coming into their homes.

It took three attempts before the conservatory was completed to satisfaction, not because they were not ready or poor at construction work, but because the rabbits had never created a hot room before and their uncertainness meant that they kept moving the glass pieces around. A few of the buckshells complained about the constant reconstruction but Maribel told them to be patient.

The next year was spent developing the mud banks for growing the strawberry seeds, inherited by their ancestors, as well as deciding when the best time of the year was to make jams. It was a wonderful year and all the buckshells' felt happy with their new jobs and excited about eating their dearest fruit, at any time of the year! Little did the rabbits know, that a black eagle had discovered their strawberry fields. The eagle, Queen Reina, along with King Roman, met many times at the Strawberry Felds. They held meetings here when no one was around, and it would become the site for some shocking news tomorrow.

CHAPTER 5

The Boars Did Not Expect This

Thursday, Evening.

The Oakash Water Diggers sensed that there was something different about the muddy earth as they burrowed their way to the canal. It almost felt like the dirt was sacred and it should be left alone. There were countless barriers on the way to the water tip such as tree trunks and mucky areas filled with heavy soil and pebbles. The badgers found worms which was a delightful surprise for them, especially since they realised that their main food source had been crawling deeper to avoid the rains. The badgers kept stopping to snack and had to give each other reminders to continue digging!

The darkness was quite hard for Agent Sol as he did not have the best sense of smell but he had the hugest appetite of them all, so he relied on Sparrowsky to move in the direction of the water. As the badgers got close to the water they stopped and stomped the wall in the direction of their friends. Stomping in counts of three, then two, was a signal that the badgers were reaching the water's edge. As Winstone and Llama waited for an indication from Sparrowsky that his left burrowers had reached the edge, they began discussing the topic of Venus. Venus had decided to make a home with Trekker because he was less of a hoarder and did not have the little ones running around him as Llama did. Although Llama liked Venus, he was in love with Honeycot and was not in the least bit disappointed when Venus went to live with Trekker.

Bonobos, Figs, Tanto, Santiago, Sparrowsky, Agent Sol, Winstone, and Llama all reached the edge of the muddy banks and created little holes for the river water to flow through. As the badgers made their way back through the tunnels that they had dug, they saw a light that grew stronger as they got closer to the exit. The boars were too scared to stop and talk about it. But no one was denying that light should not be there, it was night-time after all. As the light got brighter the tunnel began to go downwards, and a strange noise could be heard, sounding like humans, but the language was unrecognisable.

As they got closer to the exit, they could see millions, if not billions of stars. The clusters were made up of assorted colours, shapes, and sizes. The Oakash Diggers marvelled at this site for they had never seen stars this closely before. They could feel the mass power of the stars and the light gave them unexpected energy. One of the nearby clusters contained unusual shades of white, yellow, and red, which meant it had gone through the process of a supernova. Santiago explained that a supernova is caused by the gravity of the star, and the nuclear fuel of the star competes with its energy; eventually, the star explodes and radiates outwards.

The startled badgers must have run for one hundred metres before they all came falling out of the end of the tunnel and landed on clouds, high above a mountainous peak. Slowly, the clouds swayed downwards, and all the Oakash Water Diggers jumped off and went to the nearest bush for cover. The badgers were so keen to land on the ground that they had not acknowledged that they were standing on clouds! They could hear children playing and laughing and speaking in a different tongue, which was the noise they heard from inside the tunnels.

As they peeked through the bushes, they could see valleys upon valleys with homes that looked like those of the humans, but much bigger, made of a foreign type of wood, and had many tools out the front. The children wore bright coloured scarves, and had dark skin, smallish eyes, and dark-coloured hair. The elders wore darker-coloured clothes but had bright wraps around their heads or necks. Suddenly, the badgers noticed that these beings had three eyes, not two. The extra eye was positioned on their forehead, above their nose and each eye was a distinct colour from their two main eyes. All the elders carried sticks when they walked through their big paddy fields. The sticks had little coloured mushrooms on them and every time the stick moved, the mushrooms released a powder into the field. Everywhere else they looked around them were thousands of white lilies.

Llama said, “Strangely, this feels like home.”

“Wow, we can see in colour now!” exclaimed Figs.

“Hooray, this is wonderful,” Tanto said. They could see everything in rich, vibrant colour, which was the first time for them because badgers only ever saw things in black and white. But the enthusiasm was quickly replaced with confusion because they could not understand how they had arrived in this strange place.

Both Figs and Agent Sol looked at each other and

said, "let's explore!"

"No, let me go!" said Sparrowsky, "I'm the fittest, so let me go," and he went a few metres ahead and was joined by his burrow partner Agent Sol.

As Sparrowsky and Agent Sol began to explore on their own, they froze on the spot.

"What could be the matter?" asked Llama, as the boars caught them up.

Llama and Tanto approached Sparrowsky and Agent Sol, and they froze too. In front of them were two men who looked Tibetan, sitting inside a wooden hut, resting on chairs. Except these chairs were made of wood which had little branches that moved and morphed into unrecognisable fishes. These chairs were alive!

The men were playing a type of card game, but with stones with markings on them. There was a fish that was hanging in the air with no strings between the two men. The fish looked like a silver, dead cod with spikey tentacles. The boars looked closer at the fish; it had a small blunt knife in the back of it, but the cod was not bleeding or in any pain. As the two men spoke to the fish and smiled at it, one of them took the blade out of the fish, and suddenly, it became a man. The man appeared out of thin air! The two other men continued smiling, and so did the fish man. It was like they were playing a game, and the person who was losing had to become the fish. This blunt knife transformed the man into something else. As the game went on, another man had the blunted knife put into his neck and he became a fish too, but he was a turquoise and pink fish with fins that hung 30 centimetres below it. The badgers were mesmerised by the game and watched them play for 50 minutes before they realised that they needed to focus on exploring the area.

Later, a local wise woman would inform the boars that the fish-man was transporting to a star and fighting hideous birds. The men were great warriors and had fought in battles with scavenger birds from another galaxy. Eventually, the badgers became very aware of how hungry they were, and Sparrowsky with Agent Sol continued their food search.

"This is a strange place; how did we get here and how do we get home?" asked Winstone. Winstone was one of the younger boars and was missing his home. He remembered he had brought his compass with him, so he searched for it, but it was not in his backpack. He had hoped that the compass would help them to find out where they were. Llama felt he needed to calm Winstone and the others by reassuring his friend, "Where there's a will there is a way."

The boars stood in amazement at the billions of stars above them. The sight was spectacular!

"Where are we?" asked Llama.

"We could be in Finland, or the North Pole, or..." hesitated Bonobos.

"Where Bonobos, just say where," said Llama in a calm voice.

"Inside a galaxy," said Bonobos quietly, his eyes barely looking up because he felt ashamed of what he had said. It was so bizarre to consider that they were anywhere else other than Oakash. They had not travelled in a cabin, or left Oakash for several months, so where were they?

After the boars ate a bunch of berries, which may not have been berries but smelt like them, they settled next to each other under a huge hibiscus grove and fell asleep. It was a cool night; the sky was bright with stars and the temperature dropped a bit. The badgers awoke to see enormous birds, which looked like condors, flying above them, and purple bats hovering in circles. They also saw two men standing and watching a large fire near the paddy fields. They held large sticks with pointed edges, as if ready to fight a threat to their paddy fields.

As the night drew on, the sky turned a turquoise to purple colour, but it was not just in the sky, it was all around them. It even made the boars look multi-coloured. One of the brightest stars called Antares appeared like the sun, with golden orange colour which turned a darker red, and you could see the solar flares firing out of it and leaving glares in the sky. The glares took a long time to fully dissipate. It affected the moods of the boars, making them feel tired and resentful. Soon the men, women, and children were out on the paddy fields and near the water well, chanting in large chains, holding hands. The boars could not understand what they were seeing or hearing, but it felt like they were chanting to protect Antares. A group of natives looked like they were crying, and some of the people had serious faces, whilst others looked confused.

Soon the boars all stood together and understood that they were in a place of strange beauty but there was an underlying omnipresence of power here, one that they could not explain. It was as if their speech had now failed them, and they were not able to bring up the topic of how to get home. Winstone eventually made a gargling noise to try and create space in his throat as he felt it had become trapped with the air of this place. He said quickly with a deep croaky voice, "Does anyone see that bridge over there with those glowing berries?"

CHAPTER 6

The Eagle and the Ace-Portal

Friday morning, 27th March.

The Oakash Water Diggers had not arrived back. It was the morning after the Oakash Water Diggers had met in the Mulberry Cave, and Blossom and her best friend Autumn were both worried that the eight-counsel members had not returned since digging for a water hole last evening. It had been more than nine hours and it had become much colder outside. She knew that badgers were meticulous communicators and therefore something was not right.

"Where are they and why have not they arrived home yet?" asked Autumn.

"I wish I knew where they were and were home now, maybe they are on the tunnel express to one of the Stops," but even as Blossom said this, her gut told her that they were not in a cabin but instead, there was danger around them.

"We must call the boars and sows to an emergency meeting now," said Autumn. She was married to Santiago and could not bear thinking that something horrible had happened to him. Autumn remembered that she had met a wonderful black eagle called Thoric almost two years ago at a travel cabin stop which could talk to animals. She wondered if she could find out where the eagle was by making inquiries at the Find my Friend Stop. This Stop was only three hours away on the Berry Bees Express.

"Blossom, why don't you call the meeting by ringing the bell and writing the time and place for the meeting?" asked Autumn.

"I can and I will... what are you up to Autumn?" asked Blossom. She could see that Autumn was planning something because she looked pensive.

"I was thinking... I am going on the Berry Bees Express to Find my Friend Stop, to ask for the whereabouts of the talking eagle, Thoric. If we can speak to the eagle, then we can ask her to find our missing friends and family," said Autumn nervously. She had decided she would go on the express immediately, even though a sow would normally ask permission from all the other sows first, especially the camp leaders Harper and Oscar. Autumn knew she would come under a great deal of scrutiny from her colony when she returned from the journey.

"Autumn!" said Blossom loudly to stop Autumn from drifting off with her thoughts. "You go now, and I will arrange the sow-boar meeting. Please be careful my dear friend, I will worry about you."

"I will be fine, Blossom. Thank you for always thinking about others, even while you are making us laugh," said Autumn. She felt glad to be taken out of her pensive mood. "I will ring the bell four times upon my return and alert the others. Bye for now, my friend," said Autumn as she brushed her tail with her good friend, Blossom.

Blossom knew it took about three hours to arrive at Find my Friend Stop, and then another three hours to return, plus two to three hours of waiting for an answer if she arrived during the opening hours. So, Blossom realised it would be at least another seven to ten hours before Autumn would return from her trip. She secretly prayed that Thoric would be willing and available to help her to find their missing friends and that the Oakash Water Diggers were safe. Blossom hurried along the various levels of her community and arrived at the massive reception area where the main fire, which heated all the homes, was lit. She saw the large mud area where she could write a message using the wooden pencil made by the badgers from a chestnut tree. Badgers sometimes pretended to write like humans. Blossom scribed where Autumn had gone and the time of her departure.

The Oak Tree Ace-Portal

The oak tree where the badgers lived underneath, was one of the tunnel express stops. It was called 'Oak Tree Ace-Portal'. No one knew why the travel cabins were called Ace-Portal and if someone tried to discover its history, then you would need to go back fifty-five-thousand-plus years. Autumn walked very quickly onto the outdoor grass. She loved it up here because you could see the sun and smell grass everywhere. She could feel her heart racing as she walked to the edge of the oak tree and looked up. She began climbing up the tree, using the branches to hang onto when she could feel her back legs losing grip on the tree. She looked up and saw that she had to climb at least another thirty feet before reaching the tunnel entrance.

Finally, Autumn saw the secret entrance and began to get more energy. She hurried up to the tunnel entrance and placed her nose on the secret key lock. The key lock was made of sensors that could read if the animal trying to enter the tunnel, was a real badger or just an unlucky and confused animal. If the sensor detected an animal that was not a badger, it would send an electric shock to scare them away. The electric shock was not painful, but it was enough to stop an animal from sniffing around the tree.

"I must make this journey and ask Thoric for help. Ace-Portal, take me to Thoric," said Autumn aloud. She waited for the sensor to detect her badger cells and then heard the tunnel elevator inside begin to turn on. Suddenly, a door of about 0.8 metres by a 1-metre wide opened. It was made of oak wood, with an electric mechanism to help it open and close. The clever badgers had improved all the tunnel doors over the last thirty years. After the great disaster with the white rabbit which had managed to get into the tunnel in 1752, badgers had been guarding the tunnel entrances in groups of three, so they would not get too bored or could take turns to sleep. The badgers constructed the cabins into machines that shrunk to the size of a grape. The small size of the cabin allowed the badgers to travel through the earth, undetected.

The badgers who guarded the tunnel entrances for the last five and a half centuries were called Badger Guards. But after recent improvements in technology and electrical engineering lessons for the badgers who had to pass rigorous tests for this course, the badgers had made the doors safer and more modern. There was no need for any Badger Guards anymore; this was good because badgers found this job boring and preferred to be in the comfort of their nests. There were about ten thousand tunnel entrances around the world, in different trees or caves. The most famous cave tunnel called Padgercan was in Pakistan. It was most famous because it is the biggest cave where conferences were held every year to celebrate Badger Achievements and share food. No human or other animal had ever set foot in this cave, and it was the safest place for the badgers from around the world to meet up.

THE FATE OF THE CONSTELLATIONS

CHAPTER 7

The Unordinary Bird and Rabbit

Late Morning, Friday.

Thoric had been alive for almost four and a half centuries, hundreds of which she had spent in Tuscany because of the great weather and its connection to the Renaissance. On this day, 29th March 2020, Thoric was at the 'Find my Friend' stop in Spain. She had been in this part of the world for the best part of ten years. This is where she met Autumn the badger about twenty moons ago and made a good friend for life. Thoric had been thinking about the badgers and how Little Bobbin had a better life because of them.

On this morning, Thoric arrived early at her post because she had not slept well. Upon her arrival, Autumn was sleeping behind the glass door by the Ace-Portal exit. 'How long had she been there?' thought Thoric. As she entered the room the lights came on automatically and Autumn was alerted. Autumn opened her eyes and smiled as soon as she saw Thoric.

“Hello, Thoric... so happy to see you! How have you been?” asked Autumn. She sounded incredibly happy but Thoric detected a slight nervousness in her voice.

“Autumn *squawk* it’s been a long time my friend... so glad you are *squawk* here,” said Thoric. Thoric squawked often when she spoke.
“I come to you with a grave concern," said Autumn whose face had become sullen.
“*Squawk* what concern you say?” asked Thoric.
“My partner Santiago has disappeared along with seven other badgers. They left last night to clear some of the river embankment so we could reach the berries and worms. It has been a chilly winter, and all are hungry,” said Autumn with a gulp in her throat.
“And then what happened *squawk**squawk*?” asked Thoric.

“We do not know anything else other than the group called themselves the Oakash Water Diggers, they travelled in twos and planned to dig four holes near the canal, there was a danger of drowning, and they never came back... I do not believe they drowned; a badger always knows when one of their own has passed on to the spirit land. I saw Blossom this morning and she agreed that I should ask for your help. Badgers never stay away from their camp for long. They had not reported back last night even though the temperature dropped below 4 Celsius. This job would not take more than five hours and they are still not home," said Autumn. She was pacing the large Stop room.

"How I help badgers?" squawked Thoric.

"I know you met the white rabbit, is his name Cosmo?" said Autumn. She was about to continue when Thoric squawked, "Cosimo, yes I know him very well, we friends for centuries now."

"Can you find him for us please... he is the only one that can connect the rabbits and badgers. Even though he is a rabbit, he has all the characters of every animal species. Cosimo could speak to one of the rabbit colonies and ask them to help dig up the passageways which the badgers made last night. Rabbits dig faster than us and they could rescue the Oakash Diggers, the counsel members who went to find food. There is something which tells me that the rabbits will play an important role in saving Santiago and my friends. Cosimo is a mystical animal and you once told me that he has the gift of prophecy. I believe he would tell me what to do," Autumn said with a huge plea in her voice.

"Yes *squawk*, I can find Cosimo. But the badgers and rabbits have not spoken for many years."

"The rabbits and badgers haven't been friends for a very long time and I think this is an opportunity to release any negative opinions. Once upon a time, we used to drink teas together," pleaded Autumn.

Autumn need not have pleaded as Thoric had sensed something was changing on Planet Earth and the white rabbit was very mystical. Had Thoric known strange activity had been occurring at Oakash, she would have gone to the white rabbit herself. Although Cosimo hardly spoke to anyone nowadays as he was often in a reclusive state. Cosimo would look into your eyes and it seemed like the stars were swirling in his eyes. It was like the stars made words that had sounds, and these star words would move into your bones and give you a message.

"Oh, my goodness!" squawked Thoric aloud.

"What, what?" asked Autumn quickly as she was taken back by Thoric's outburst.

"Cosimo said to me *squawk* years ago that I would 'bridge'*squawk* the badgers with rabbits, I did not know what *squawk* Cosimo meant. My God *squawk* it is time for me to bridge the creatures... how did *squawk* Cosimo know that you would ask this of me lunations ago? *squawk* *squawk*. Cosimo is prophetic, he can know things decades before they happen *squawk*," she bellowed with a shiver down her feathers.

"Thoric, this is destiny. Do not worry, if anything, a bridge is what got us into problems in the first place so things cannot get any worse, can they?" Autumn asked.

Thoric then remembered that the white rabbit had been spending time in Canada.

"I know to find Cosimo *squawk*, he is in Burlington *squawk* and there is an Ace-Portal at Maple tree, rabbits do not know about it except Little Bobbin," she breathed in quickly as she was speaking so fast. "I leave now *squawk*... one of the badgers not working *squawk* can come here... I will send a message to Otto now so he can start the shift earlier."

Autumn went back to Ashdown Forest to report back to the counsel, and what Thoric had said she would do to help the Oakash Water Diggers. This was coming together well; Thoric had agreed to help the badgers, and Cosimo was in Burlington of all places. Burlington was known amongst the badger kingdom to house the most organised and diligent rabbits. This was not a coincidence, it was synchronicity because she knew, in her gut, that things were falling into place; and there was no such thing as coincidence.

The White Rabbit

Cosimo and Thoric have known each other for thousands of full moons, shooting stars and supernovas. They were from the same era, the Renaissance. The greatest artists had all been competing to be the most successful seller and to be famous all around the world. Everyone had become obsessed with artwork, including all the art technicians, the people who made the paints, and the wealthy buyers. Cosimo came out of the Titian painting, the Rabbit of the Madonna, on the morning of the same day as Thoric came out of the Milky Way painting by Tintoretto. Cosimo travelled to Tintoretto's art studio to find Thoric because he knew that she would also be transported out of the painting. Cosimo was gifted with the ability to see into the future.

They first met outside Tintoretto's art studio and

became good friends. They both learned to speak in English as well as twelve other tongues during their travels. After learning to communicate in the human language, they could communicate with animals and creatures. Both took it upon themselves to learn to speak more languages and practise with the schools in the badger, rabbit, deer, lizard, and alpaca communities. Cosimo had barely spent time with Thoric in the last 50 years because their time to destroy the black holes had not yet come to fruition.

Cosimo knew of what was to come and felt compelled to keep it quiet until the right time. Although Cosimo forgot that he had told Thoric he would be living hidden near the badger and rabbit community, learning about the animal's habitat there and how they survived the wintry conditions.

Cosimo knew that Thoric would be arriving soon to ask for help. He knew that rabbits would freely offer to help the badgers despite their differences. He would take an Ace-Portal to Oakash after Thoric left, so he could travel on his own and enhance his prophecy abilities. The only thing that Cosimo could not predict, was what would happen in the Milky Way. He knew the stars were misaligning since Tintoretto's painting altered when Thoric came out of the canvas. He also knew the world had changed too much. This world was not anchored. Somehow, humans had forgotten how to breathe and live. This human contagion and the paintings had triggered something inside the Milky Way where black holes would separate the stars and become swallowed up by them. This would cause a catastrophic effect on planet earth.

Cosimo started thinking, 'The artists of the Renaissance had changed the landscape of the art world, and there was magic in the air. Little did they know that their paints had developed a magical spell. They had inadvertently caused their paints to become potent. It was like a witch had put a spell on the paints to bring the painting alive. Soon, I will see Thoric, and we will be together again. I was given the gift of insight and I knew what was to be done. But I do not know the outcome as this will be determined by the next few days,' he thought to himself. 'The question I have is, where are the other animals from the Renaissance paintings? I was always curious; why did Thoric and I come out of the painting and not all the other animals... or did they also come out? Both Thoric and I had visited the National Gallery, in London, many times, to find out if other animals had escaped, but we could not tell if this had happened to any other bird, sea creature, amphibian, or animal'.

CHAPTER 8

The Milky Way is Way Stranger than Imagined

Friday afternoon, 27th March.

Earth

Billions of humans stopped in front of their homes, on the scaffolding of London, in their cars, observatories, on beaches, deserts, coffee shops, schools, and looked out at the Milky Way. What they saw left them shocked and scared. The Milky Way looked like it was being pulled towards something. Never had humans seen the Milky Way so bright during the day. The colours of the sky on earth began changing from a shade of light pink to a darker shade of garden pink, to rose.

Observatories around the world like the one in Chile called La Silla Observatory had stopped their work and were now focused on the stars in the Milky Way and the strange happenings there. Major charities were on high alert and speaking to the WHO, UNICEF, Amnesty International, and other non-profit organisations. Humans stopped for the first time in years. What were they seeing thousands of light years away; and how had the sky colour changed?

Oakash, afternoon.

Autumn returned to Oaktree Ace-Portal on the same Friday day, seven hours after she had left to ask Thoric for help. Autumn rang the bell from the top as promised to Blossom. Thoric was already on her way to Canada to speak to Cosimo. It was mid-afternoon and Autumn could sense that the energy had changed in her community. She was feeling very tired and looking at the view downwards to the bottom of the oak tree made her feel even more exhausted.

As Autumn descended the large oak tree, she could see badgers, bats, deer, adders, wood mice, rabbits, and other animals for miles. They were all staring up at the sky. She stopped midway down the tree and held tightly onto one of the branches as she looked up at the sky. As Autumn stared, she gasped. The Milky Way was separating apart and heading in different directions. One star called UY Scuti seemed to be bending towards something. 'Could it be a black hole?' she wondered to herself.

CHAPTER 9

Little Bobbin

Friday afternoon.

Little Bobbin met up with Laurel at the Amazon River which was a good socialising spot.

'After Captain Marlow calmed down from the Luna incident, I went back home to see Coco and share the maple wood I had collected that morning,' Little Bobbin thought on his way to the river. Coco was not at home so little did she know that Little Bobbin had also collected maple syrup too and hidden it so she would receive a good surprise. "Oh, to see that smile... what a great feeling," Little Bobbin told Laurel when he embraced her on the sturdy bridge. Then a thrashing sound came from above, but this was not the normal warning sign from the other comrades, it was like a crowing sound. Everyone could hear rabbits talking amongst themselves – in hushed voices saying, "she's talking to us," "where did she come from?" and "is she from outer space?". They were talking about a bird who was communicating with

King Roman.'

A new mood had arrived in the camp and the rabbits were excited. King Roman was standing at the edge of exit ninety-eight. He was partially obstructing the light which would normally shine inside the camp of the Amazon River. Amazon River was one of the largest camps in the whole community. It had three bridges and about one hundred rabbits living inside. The bridges were always busy; sometimes the rabbits would stop to talk with each other and watch the fishes in the lake underneath their feet. The rabbits had created a mini jungle inside this camp.

"How may I help you Thoric?" asked King Roman.

"Who is King Roman talking to?" asked Little Bobbin out loud.

"Why he's talking to the blackbird!" exclaimed Maribel.

"Oh, did not see you there... hello Maribel... have you been well my dear? Where is my friend?" asked Little Bobbin, but before he could finish. Maribel had already answered.
"Behind schedule, he will be kicking himself that he is not here. He had to charge the little un's to clear up the smell from the cat," said Maribel. They were talking about Captain Marlow of course-everyone knew that he and Little Bobbin were best friends.
"Shush!" said King Roman. "I cannot hear Thoric," he shouted to the camp.

Thoric appeared at the top of the exit. Her head entered the community as she sat down. A huge gasp came from the camp. No rabbit had seen a bird put its head inside a camp, let alone speak, and stand near their King.

Thoric kept squawking in between words. "I *squawk*, have news for *squawk* you King Roman *squawk* I need to *squawk* speak to you privately," said Thoric.

"Let's meet in the strawberry fields," said King

Roman. All the rabbits looked around in confusion because they had never heard of the Strawberry Fields, except the buckshells'. The buckshells avoided making eye contact with the buckshots so they would not give their hidden secret away; the female rabbits had all been sworn to secrecy to Queen Reina. Thoric quickly turned around as if she knew where to go.

"How does Thoric know where strawberry fields are?" asked Maribel's friend, Twinkle.

"He's been there before," said Maribel, looking at Little Bobbin as if she had just received an epiphany.
Little Bobbin had met Thoric before and knew that things were about to change in their camp.

King Roman, Queen Reina, and Little Bobbin Talk to Thoric

Thoric had shown Little Bobbin how to travel through the badger Ace-Portal so that he could go to one of the best rabbit communities in the world. Thoric had helped Little Bobbin cross the badger tunnels to this camp and the badgers pretended that they had not seen him. Little Bobbin had met Thoric when he was a captive. Thoric had been a regular visitor where he was a captive and was surprised that the dark bird could speak his language. It was not until Little Bobbin was sunbathing outside that he realised that the bird could speak to him. Little Bobbin moaned daily about the other animals and how noisy they were when he was outside playing in the garden.

"There are too many of us here. I wish I could join a colony with other rabbits," groaned Little Bobbin.

"I can take you to a good home, yes, the best rabbit place in the world," squawked Thoric.

"But how, I am a captive, and I cannot leave this

home?" asked Little Bobbin.

"Why do you not dig, silly rabbit?" smiled Thoric.

"It would take years for me to dig on my own. The ground here is very hard and full of tree roots, and the fences are five feet under. The meerkats are always digging over there but it is too small a spot to escape from," grumbled Little Bobbin. He would moan at the animals who lived with him, but they would shrug off his complaints. Thoric would visit the garden and eat the food that the humans would leave outside for the birds

But now, Little Bobbin ran to the strawberry fields, even though Coco had warned him not to.

"Don't go! You are just interfering again." Coco shouted at Little Bobbin, knowing he would ignore her.

"Byeee my love... surprise! I left some maple syrup in the bowl," Little Bobbin shouted back at his wife, as he took a different route to the Strawberry Fields.

Coco smiled at her partner and turned as he took off down a path that only he would know, and no one else.

King Roman arrived at Strawberry Fields where Thoric was waiting for him. Queen Reina and the uninvited Little Bobbin arrived thirty seconds after the King. King Roman acknowledged Little Bobbin and smiled at his Queen. Thoric recognised Little Bobbin straight away and they greeted each other very warmly. The King and Queen of Oakash knew all about their history; it was because of Thoric that Little Bobbin could join the Burlington camp even though he had never lived in a rabbit community before.

"My friend Autumn met me today at the 'Find my Friend' stop. She was upset because *squawk* her partner has been missing along with *squawk* seven friends since last night *squawk*," said Thoric before the King interrupted.

"Autumn, who is Autumn, Thoric?" asked the inquisitive King.

"My King, please let Thoric finish what he wants to say," Queen Reina smiled at the eager rabbit.

"Autumn is my friend as I said *squawk* why you ask?" Thoric asked the King.

"I did not know you had many rabbit friends, Thoric," said Queen Reina.

"She is no rabbit *squawk*, she badger, from England," said Thoric bemused. Thoric knew that rabbits and badgers had never settled their differences since the disaster of 1752.

"A badger?" asked King Roman.

"Yes, *squawk* badger. You not speaking particularly good English today rabbits," said Thoric mocking them, but also a little annoyed because the rabbits were delaying Thoric from delivering an important message.

"I met Autumn briefly when she let me use the cabin to come to Burlington. She pretended she did not see me so that I could be free to travel alone," said Little Bobbin. "If it was not for Autumn, the other badgers would have stopped me from travelling on the cabins," he continued.

"Continue Thoric, and I apologise for our questions... you know our history," said Queen Reina.

"Badger, badger *squawk* want your help. Badger *squawk* Autumn said her colony sent eight badgers to the bridge to create a flood by the water, so they *squawk* could reach their food. Very hungry are the badgers, and cold in England *squawk*, and moody the *squawk* badgers are when hungry and cold," said Thoric. She thought to herself that this was the longest sentence she had been able to speak to the rabbits. "She needs your *squawk**squawk* help," continued Thoric.

All rabbits looked shocked and kept quiet. "You *squawk* help badgers now," said Thoric.

"But how? I mean what do you mean... what does Autumn need, why us?" asked King Roman.

"Yes, how can we help the badgers?" asked Little Bobbin.

"You are to travel *squawk* to the Milky Way *squawk*." Little Bobbin fainted. He remembered his dream from last night.

CHAPTER 10

The Planet of the Lilies

Friday morning, 27th March.

Bonobos, Figs, Tanto, Santiago, Sparrowsky, Agent Sol, Winstone, and Llama all lay on their backs and stared upwards. They could see that the stars had been slowly, very slowly, moving towards a black object in the sky. The boars did not know if the stars were circling towards this black object, or if the stars were hiding behind it. The turquoise sky had changed to a rose-pink colour, like a pink shade from a Renaissance painting.

Something was vastly different about this place. "This looks like we are in the centre of the Milky Way, but I know this sounds crazy... I can see Antares and KW Sagittarii," said Sparrowsky. Agent Sol ran towards the turquoise-red coloured berries on his own, being so independent and brave.

"It seems like it Sparrowsky; I saw a documentary from the British Broadcasting Corporation program about the universe in the transport cabins," said Santiago. The other badgers all nodded their heads in agreement. Badgers knew that Santiago was serious about the Milky Way because he would often say how much he wanted to buy a telescope to watch the stars at night. Winstone was also an aficionado of the Milky Way, but he knew truly little about Renaissance paintings.

"But how did we get here, and why are we here?" asked Sparrowsky, confused and tired.

"We must have travelled here from the tunnel we dug. It must have been under a spell that we knew nothing about," answered Llama.

"Magic tunnels, the Milky Way, this is like a dream except it's not," said Winstone.

Santiago was noticeably quiet since arriving in the new land. He was very much into creature comforts. "I have heard that paintings could come alive and that the Renaissance was a strange time because artists had complained of images going missing from their paintings, especially animals. Can you believe this? I heard this from Autumn who had spoken to a talking birdie. This bird was very friendly, and she, yes, she, a female bird, told Autumn that she had appeared out of a canvas," said Santiago in disbelief at what he was saying.

Santiago had been thinking about Autumn and whether she had gone to ask Thoric for help. He knew that Autumn was very inquisitive, and intelligent and would be thinking about how Thoric could help gain insight into his disappearance. Agent Sol came running back with a huge bunch of turquoise-red berries in his backpack.

"Time for our snacks... we have eaten more now than in the last two weeks. I wonder how everyone at home is doing and whether they know we are missing," said Figs.

Figs, being the quietest of the badgers, had not spoken once since arriving on the Milky Way. He had been contemplating what the fish game was all about. He was secretly enjoying being on another planet and eating their delicious berries. He spent a good deal of time on his own, even though he was partnered with Floral and shared a home.

"Agreed," said all the other badgers in

synchronicity.

"I wonder why the Oakash Diggers are here. Something is not okay on this planet. The stars are moving toward that black object which we cannot see. The sky changes colour and we can see colour for the first time. The people here look like they are chanting to save the planet. What should we do here on this planet?" questioned Figs.

The badgers sat silently and took in every word that Figs was saying. Figs must have been thinking about the badger's purpose on the Milky Way for him to speak in this unusual outburst.

"Look up!" said Winstone and Tanto abruptly. All the badgers stared up. What they saw was so out of the ordinary: two small celestial figures appeared in the sky. As the two individuals got closer, it was clear to the badgers that they were the size of a human but had the features of painted artwork during the Renaissance era.

Santiago knew who these figures were as he was Tintoretto's second biggest badger fan. Jupiter (God of the sky, also known as Zeus) and Juno (guardian of her state) were flying above them and moving in every direction. Juno was partially naked but covered in silky white sheets; she was a very pale white colour with brownish hair. Jupiter had a very muscular body, olive-skinned, handsome but slightly frightening; he was also semi-naked but had most of his torso covered in a red and blue sheet. Jupiter and Juno moved so fast.

Juno kept squirting milk from her breast and lilies would grow where the milk landed on the ground. Therefore, this celestial sphere got the 'Planet of the Lilies' name from Juno's milk. Jupiter looked confused and angry. He was trying to find someone. His son, Hercules.

Suddenly, the four angels from Tintoretto's painting appeared in the sky. The angels' wings were white in some parts, and other parts of their wings had pink, blue, and green colours. The iridescent colours of the wings created wonderful rainbows behind them, which took different shapes; some were semi-oval, whilst the other rainbows were shaped into circles. One of the angels flew towards Juno and held a torch for her while she flew away from Jupiter. Juno was upset with Jupiter about something important, so the angels were sending her happiness. Jupiter was speaking to her and throwing his arms around in the air. Juno was not paying him much attention, instead, she flew away from Jupiter.

Whilst the badgers sat up in bewilderment at what they were witnessing, the flying characters all disappeared behind UY Scuti and then were gone from their vision. Bonobos wondered how the two strange individuals could disappear so easily behind these stars. It was the most impressive sight, and the badgers were in awe of this place.

“What did we just witness?” asked Tanto in shock.

“We just saw characters from Tintoretto’s painting. But Hercules was not with them, and I do not know where he could be. Is it possible that Jupiter is looking for him?” Santiago explained what he had studied as he sat up.

"The peacocks and crab must be around here somewhere. As the legend goes, Juno was not the mother of Hercules so she may be trying to get away from Jupiter. I remember now what happened. Jupiter wanted to make Hercules immortal so he took his half-mortal son to his partner Juno to drink from her breast because it was believed that her milk could make babies immortal. But, as Hercules began to breastfeed, Juno woke up and her milk came out very quickly, which then created the Milky Way," replied Santiago.

"Ooohhh," said Bonobos.

"That would explain why Jupiter looks angry, he is looking for his son and could be blaming Juno for his disappearance. Of course, I am just speculating," continued Bonobos.

"Is it true, that Juno created the Milky Way? Or is it mythology?" asked Winstone.

"It is said that the story is just folklore, but I like to think that Juno created the constellations," replied Santiago. Santiago thought to himself, how proud Autumn would be of his answer, helped immensely by his education. Santiago only studied Renaissance because Autumn had met Thoric. Santiago began drawing the painting of the Origin of the Milky Way on the mud so everyone could glimpse what this painting looked like. The other badgers stood around, eager to see what intricacies the painting consisted of.

"Maybe we should look for Hercules," suggested Llama.

"Could the strange movement of the stars be associated with these characters from the painting?" asked Sparrowsky.

"It is possible, Sparrowsky. I think we should find Hercules so he can stop Jupiter from feeling angry and maybe he can help us go back home to Badgercom. What does everyone think?" questioned Llama.

"This is a good idea. I am scared... and I feel ashamed to admit this to you all. Where do we start, and can we take berries with us?" replied Agent Sol but with more questions. Agent Sol was always thinking with his belly.

"We are all frightened, my dear Agent Sol. We are in unknown territory and are yet to meet anyone who can help us. Yes, Agent Sol, let us fill our backpacks with berries. And we could start by asking one of the people in the village below," said Bonobos.

"Good plan Bonobos. Agent Sol and Figs, please collect enough berries to fill our sacks. And Tanto,

Winstone, and Sparrowsky, go down to the nearest village and see if there are any obstacles in our way, like traps or rivers. Santiago, you stay on guard with Bonobos and me," ordered Llama. Llama was emerging into the leader that Honeycot inspired him to be. He felt hugely confident and proud of his new group.

Agent Sol and Figs scurried towards the nearest bushes, filled their bags with food and quickly returned. Figs and Agent Sol emptied their bags of berries, gave the fruits to Llama, Bonobos, and Santiago, and then went back to the bushes to retrieve more berries. Llama and Bonobos stood on their hind legs so they could keep a protective eye on the three badgers who were sniffing out any dangers. By the time Figs and Agent Sol had returned with berries which would be enough for everyone and last them each four days, the other three badgers were on their way back.

Saturday Morning

The three badgers who went to look for any obstacles had been missing since last night but they arrived to join the others. Tanto was first to arrive back to the pack, followed by Winstone and Sparrowsky. They were all out of breath and lay on their backs to rest. Agent Sol and Figs began filling their bags with berries. "Up please, we do not have time to rest. I know you must be tired, but we must know what you saw," demanded Bonobos.

All three badgers sat on their bottoms and both Winstone and Sparrowsky looked at Tanto.

"Tell them!" Winstone insisted of Tanto.

"We met an older woman; she looked like she came from the South-Asian community to me but her third eye kept moving across her forehead. She could not speak any English. She saw us coming and opened her home door to let us in. She put water in bowls and lay it before our feet. She then showed us paintings that she had been drawing. She had thousands in her home. They were all different versions of the Tintoretto painting of the Origin of the Milky Way, similar to the picture Santiago just scribed on the mud. She kept pointing to one painting," said Tanto.

"What was in the painting?" asked Sparrowsky.

"It was a painting of the Milky Way as it is now.

We know this because she painted a black thing, which is what we have been seeing. She also painted Hercules who has morphed into an adult - he is no longer a baby. He was inside the UY Scuti star with humans from planet earth. The UY Scuti star is the largest of all the stars, which she drew inside her painting. We could identify Hercules because she had drawn the Origin of the Milky Way, but it was exceedingly small. She showed the transition of Hercules growing from a baby to the man he is now. This woman kept pointing towards the UY Scuti star. She kept saying, 'Nochi tar', and making impressions of us walking towards UY Scuti," continued Tanto.

"But how does she suppose we get there?" asked Santiago.

"She gave us this," said Figs who held out a piece of crystal rock. The rock was not sharp or smooth, nor was it just one colour. The crystal glowed and contained a mix of assorted colours, but it would change when you moved it around. The colours and crevices kept changing every twenty seconds.

"She kept showing us this crystal rock and pointing to UY Scuti. She was pretending to rub the stone," he continued. "My guess is, is that if we

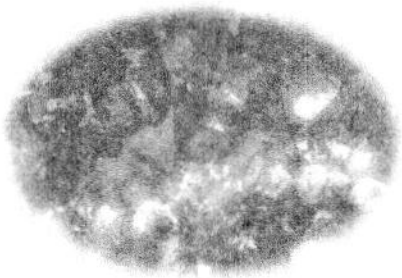

rub this stone, it will take us to the star."

As the badgers pondered how to rub the crystal, whether they all had to touch it at the same time, or if they could all go together. Unexpectedly, they heard badger's footsteps a few hundred feet away. Badgers could spot the shuffle of their kind, but they were not sure if they could hear the footsteps of rabbits too, who sounded a lot closer. Suddenly, a grand eagle came towards them and said "*Squawk* help is coming badgers *Squawk*!"

The badgers were all in shock. Santiago had a gut feeling that this bird was Thoric. The black eagle was speaking to them in a language they could speak, but even more shocking was what the bird said next. "Me Thoric from Milky Way painting *squawk* and I come with rabbits. You surprised badgers... we make friends now *squawk*" chirped Thoric.

The badgers began to sing one of their most loved poems:

Over the bridge, she goes,

She goes and follows the angel's bows,
The bows point to this land,
Land of lilies from an above hand,
Hands of nature that created this crest,
The crest of lilies from her bosom's chest.

CHAPTER 11

The Rabbits Travel at Warp Speed

Friday 27th March, late afternoon to evening.

Thoric was well known amongst the elder badger population. It was Thoric who helped the badgers plan the improved safety of the Ace-Portals around the world. There were drawings of Thoric in the badger archives, at the 'Find my History' stop. Thoric enjoyed spending time with the badgers because of their high intelligence.

Since Thoric was the oldest bird on earth, she had gained a vast amount of knowledge throughout her life. She knew that badgers disliked rabbits and that rabbits were not keen on badgers either. Thoric did not care for disputes so she thought the badgers would prefer to be surprised, rather than expect the arrival of the Burlington rabbits. Cosimo took a separate cabin to Oakash because he needed to be on his own.

Once Thoric saw Little Bobbin at the strawberry fields, she knew that he would be a great asset for the mission to the Milky Way. Little Bobbin did not hesitate to help, he was such an inquisitive and adventurous rabbit. As soon as Thoric had finished speaking about Cosimo, his prophecy, Autumn, and the story about the missing badgers, and how the badgers needed their help, Little Bobbin immediately told them about his dream, and said,

"I'm joining you dear friend. I need to help!"

Queen Reina smiled because she knew how helpful a rabbit he was. Both the King and Queen giggled when Little Bobbin started jumping around for joy because he was going on a quest. He was caring, kind, and supremely courageous and would do well on this mission.

King Roman hesitated to help Thoric because he was concerned about the safety of his colony, so it took quite some persuasion to change his mind.

Queen Reina said, "take ten rabbits with you and bring them back safely to us. You do not know how much they mean to us here." Thoric reassured her.

Eight hundred and eighty-seven rabbits volunteered to join the mission, which was too much because the cabins could fit a maximum of ten rabbits, the equivalent of eight badgers. Thoric thought how more adventurous rabbits were in comparison to the homely badgers who enjoyed staying within their camps. She liked the speed that they made decisions and how eager they were to go on a mission that came with great peril.

Ten rabbits were chosen for the quest, nine of them by Captain Marlow because of his position within the monarchy. Captain Lincoln was a fantastic leader and had great depth in his character. He could be lenient, but with an air of authority so none of the little un's ever dared test him. Hopper was the fastest of the rabbits and had won every racing competition in their yearly Olympiads. Patchy was extremely adventurous and great at seizing opportunities, such as the time she became one of the Team Leaders for the Amazon project. Laurel was the calmest of the rabbits and she loved to look for herbs to help with any ailments that someone needed. Laurel was also good at construction work. Harlequinn was the most organised and coordinated rabbit- it was Harlequinn who helped to create the new bridges in the Orchid's community. Blazing Star was the aid to the King and Queen and therefore was to be well-trusted in making good decisions. Rexus was the quietest of the rabbits but he had been able to encourage the rabbits from the Birchwood Tree camps in Burlington, to stop digging holes in the open fields because it was attracting dogs. Captain Maplelog was the most elusive of them all, in other words, he was not as well known, but his years of service proved that he would be a great asset to the adventure. No need to say more about Little Bobbin.

Thoric led the rabbits to the nearest tree with an Ace-Portal. Suddenly, the animals could see in colour which enriched their experience of their mission. They were able to see the different brown tones of the tree, the rich colour of the space around them, and the little insects became vivid.

The base of the tree was a dark brown mixed with shades of green, and fifty feet from the Ace-Portal. Little Bobbin was the only rabbit who knew about the Ace-Portals, but Thoric had asked him to never mention them when he was rescued.

“Wow!” said all the rabbits in unison.

“I’ve been on one,” said Little Bobbin. Little Bobbin could not contain his excitement about boarding an Ace-Portal again. All the other rabbits stared at him in disbelief.

“How and what? Sorry, Little Bobbin, did you say that you have been on an Ace-Portal cabin before?” asked Captain Marlow.

“Ace-Portal, yes Marlow. That is how I arrived at Burlington. I was asked to keep it secret by Thoric and our King and Queen, but I struggled to keep it private all these years. Thoric met me in the garden when I was a captive in Ottawa, and she guided me to the nearest tunnel so I could join the best rabbit community in the world. If it were not for Thoric and his friendship with our Queen and King, I would be lost and without a community,” said Little Bobbin excitedly. Then he remembered that he had just retold the story to his King and Queen knowing full well that they already knew, but his excitement sometimes made him forgetful.

Captain Marlow looked at Little Bobbin with confusion. 'How could he not tell me,' thought Captain Marlow. Then, Thoric looked at the captain and said "If he told you, *squawk* you would all be befuddled *squawk*. You rabbits are very adventurous and brave and finding cabins would make trouble."

Captain Marlow relaxed and smiled at his friend. He started to understand Little Bobbin even more and why he was so fantastical when he told stories.

"When you went in the cabin, how did you not stay the size of a grape when you came out of it?" asked Harlequinn.

"You come back to normal size "squawk" when out of the cabin," said Thoric.

"If truth be told my friends, I did not know I had shrunk," Little Bobbin said.

Thoric explained that the cabins moved at an extremely fast speed and could reach England in under four hours if she selected 'smart speed' motion on the cabin systems - it was faster than a Concorde and only a select few travellers were permitted to pick this mode. The rabbits were quiet, listening to every word and *squawk* the eagle uttered.

Thoric flew up to the centre of their beloved maple tree and asked the rabbits to follow her.

The tree was tremendous. It was huge, strong, so tall, and very old. Their claws skilfully pierced the wood as they climbed which helped to stop any motion sickness. All the climbers had to take mini breaks and sit on the branches to regain their breath. None of them had climbed a tree before except Little Bobbin who seemed very skilled at it.

At one point, the rabbits could not see where Thoric had flown because she liked to move about a lot. Again, the rabbits resumed their ascension up the tree towards Thoric.

"*Squawk* rabbits hear me! I will open the door now. Are you ready?" said Thoric from somewhere above them.

"No! We are not even twenty-five feet up yet Thoric!" shouted Captain Lincoln who was leading from the front.

Captain Lincoln and Laurel reached the tunnel entrance first. Followed by Captain Marlow and the others. Little Bobbin arrived last because he was helping the tired rabbits find the tunnel entrance. 'Three captains from three different rabbit camps, the King and Queen's aid, plus Little Bobbin, and six other rabbits seemed like a good team,' thought Thoric. Thoric had special permission to open the doors - after all, she was a VIP. She waited for the doors to open, and the sound of the electronics made the rabbits aware that the Ace-Portal cabin was opening within the tree.

A 'hiss' sound came from the Ace-Portal as the doors opened. The express cabin had glass on its exterior, with lights inside on different voltages, as well as air conditioning. The rabbits were looking at each other in bewilderment. Finally, the fate of the ambitious rabbits was shifting and what they would experience would change them forever.

"All aboard *squawk*?" asked Thoric.

"Yes, we are all accounted for Thoric. Thank you for checking that each representative is here rather than rushing ahead," said Captain Maplelog.

The rabbits could not understand how it was possible to change their size, and excitement overcame them. The lights flicked five times, and

Thoric pulled the lever and then typed in the next stop with her claws.

"Berry Bees Express to Ashdown Forest. Four hours *squawk* to the Oak Tree Ace-Portal... *squawk* watch the screen for entertainment," said Thoric. "We might arrive sooner if fewer badgers are commuting now. Traffic jams they call it when too many badgers travel," squawked Thoric.

"Magnificent," said Blazing Star.

"The badgers are ahead of our times," said Harlequinn.

"I was thinking that too," said Patchy excitedly. Captain Maplelog sat up and looked at the rabbits. He was also mesmerised by the Ace-Portal and was ready for an adventure. For the last four years, patrolling the Lotus community, he had been yearning for something more.

The cabin screen could show various documentaries and films. The badgers liked to use this time travel to learn about the universe. Thoric decided to educate the rabbits more: "We watch *squawk* the badger community in Ashdown Forest," said Thoric, "you learn about them."

"Gosh," said Rexus. The rabbits enjoyed the visuals on the screen. They had never been this close to a television box before. Little Bobbin realised that little people did not live inside the screen as he had suspected when he was a captive. The education from badgers was strangely liberating because they were able to improve their quality of life and enjoy the boundless beauty of nature such as learning to create the travel cabins using the earth's heat.

The film lasted almost two hours and thirty minutes. The rabbits were a bit bored by the end and started to yawn and snooze. They thought the badgers were a bit slow at doing tasks, for example, storing wood in their little homes took them far too long for such a simple task. The badgers refused to leave their lodges because it was colder than 5 Celsius so they did not collect wood during the filming, which didn't make sense to the rabbits because they worked at warp speed, and it was much colder in Burlington.

The rabbits learned about the first badgers to arrive at Oakash Tree Ace-Portal, a bit about the annual gathering, the food they liked, how they kept warm, and what they did for fun, such as very artistic things like painting. Thoric decided that it would be a clever idea to show the rabbits about the 'History of our Badgercom.' The rabbits were reluctant at first because they had grown weary; the last two hours and thirty minutes had gone very slowly.

"You will enjoy it," said Thoric chirpily. Blazing Star looked at Hopper as if to say, I hope so. The two rabbits smiled at each other, looked at the screen, and then at each other again.

"Incredible!" they said as the documentary began.

The Badgers Welcome the Rabbits

Friday, late afternoon to evening.

All the rabbits and even Thoric had fallen asleep during the express ride to the Oak Tree Ace-Portal. He suddenly woke up to the sound of an old badger's voice, "Ace-Portal, arriving in one minute. Countdown 60, 59, 58..."

Thoric had travelled all around the world on these tunnels so he knew that the cabin would lock itself to the great metals built into the tree upon arrival. Clink, hiss, and then the doors opened.

"We are here rabbits *squawk*," said Thoric in a sleepy voice.

As the rabbits began to step out of the cabin, one by one, their size returned to normal. The animals felt slightly disorientated and took some deep breaths to feel less dizzy. The smell of the fresh oak tree and the forest around them reminded the new guests how all animals depended on strong trees to thrive in their communities, and there were similar practices among the animal species. Perhaps it was time to leave their differences with the badgers in the past and become neighbourly again.

The rabbits looked downwards at the long way to the bottom of the tree, and each felt anxious because they could fall if they were not careful. It was slightly warmer in England compared to Canada where temperatures would fall below -30 Celsius. Thoric flew out after the last rabbit had exited and went down to the badgers, who were eagerly awaiting them at the bottom of the old tree.
"Captain Lincoln, you go first, and I will go last," said Captain Marlow.

Captain Maplelog agreed to go in the middle to give him a clear lookout in case any rabbits needed help. Hundreds of branches and leaves blocked the view of the waiting badgers, so Captain Maplelog wanted easy communication with the rabbit at the front and rear of the pack. Captain Lincoln also agreed, and all three captains rubbed their twitching noses together.

"Follow me and do as I say," ordered Captain Lincoln.

As quick as that, the captain began his descent and all the other rabbits followed closely behind. Patchy lost her footing by the midsection of the tree and squealed in fear, but thankfully there were branches everywhere to grab onto and Rexus helped Patchy to regain her pawing. Hopper, the best runner of all the rabbits, knew that his speedy skills would not stop him from falling if he did not pay attention.

It took about ten minutes for all to descend the tree because it was an enormous oak, five hundred years old or more. Patchy liked this oak tree, she recognised it, as did all the rabbits. Oak trees were incredibly old and strong, they emitted a powerful strength, protected the animals from strangers and made them feel safe. Oak trees communicated with their beloved Maple tree in Canada, and they shared water and minerals through the mushrooms deep in the earth.

As they moved towards the last ten feet of the tree, the rabbits could see hundreds of badgers everywhere. There was wood which had been carved into shapes of different leaves at the bottom, presumably for their King or Queen to walk on. The badger leaders Harper and Oscar, and eight other badgers, on either side of the leaders stood on their hind legs, four holding wooden craters between their limbs. The rabbits began to smell something quite lovely coming from near the badger's feet; fruits of all shapes and colours. All around them were wooden barrels filled with berries, nuts and seeds.

Thoric was flying around the badgers and talking to them about the colder but sunnier weather in Canada.

"Welcome to the rabbits from Burlington," squawked Thoric chirpily.

Captain Lincoln landed on the ground first. Then one by one, all the rabbits landed and had no choice but to stand on the carved wood, which it turned out, had been laid out, especially for them. The rabbits enjoyed this special treatment, and they began to feel more relaxed. The sun was going down on the forest and the sky had never glowed so brightly. The leaves of the trees looked like the colour of autumn which glistened, and a sparkling shimmer shone around Ashdown Forest which made the place look truly magical.

"Greetings to our British kingdom, to you dear rabbits," said Harper. He had a serious look on his face but tried to smile. He was thinking how odd the whole situation was and wondering if a friendship would develop between their kingdoms.

"We are so pleased you came to us," smiled Oscar to the rabbits. "At last, we are reunited! Badgers with rabbits!" Oscar was less pessimistic than Harper, but he also understood why Harper would have reservations about uniting with the bunnies. As Oscar spoke, four badgers, two from each line standing beside the camp leaders, handed out special, sweet, and tasty berries to the hungry rabbits. The rabbits all took the berries and ate them quickly. The badgers looked pleased.

"Thank you," said Captain Maplelog to Harper and Oscar.

"Where did they get all these berries from?" sniffled Little Bobbin, telepathically communicating to Blazing Star by rubbing noses with her. "Maybe the Oakash Water Diggers' plan worked, and we are not needed," she replied.

Autumn saw Little Bobbin and tried extremely hard to not scream in excitement. Little Bobbin recognised Autumn and smiled with his twitching whiskers. Autumn and Treeshoot were sitting at the end of each line. Treeshoot and the other standing badgers looked nervous and uncomfortable. Badgers did not like having to stand up on their hind legs, but this was how the badgers welcomed important guests.

As the initial welcoming party had finished, Thoric took Harper, Oscar, and the captains to an underground room where they would have privacy. Here, Thoric spent one hour telling his friends about artists from the Renaissance, about Cosimo, Hercules and how he had grown into a man and was living in the Milky Way. She told them that since the Origin of the Milky Way painting had been displaced when Thoric came out of the painting, the Milky Way galaxy was a ticking time bomb for destruction. Thoric explained that animals would not be able to see the black hole, and they would need all the rabbits and badgers' help to save the galaxy from a catastrophe.

Trudging through the busy crowd, the ten rabbits and hundreds of badgers looked up at the sky. Their attention was directed towards the Milky Way which was much more visible as the sunset settled on the horizon. Suddenly, a loud sound came from space like a crush and crunch sound. Thousands of stars, 25000 lightyears away, looked like they were about to collide. These stars were hundreds of miles apart, but their outer regions were creating gravity which increased by a million-fold, and a new black hole was emerging. This black chasm was dreadfully close to Antares which worried Thoric. This one was stronger than any other black hole ever.

CHAPTER 12

The White Rabbit Arrives

Friday, late evening.

Harper and Oscar led the counsel gathering in the badger cave, fifty metres from the Oak Tree. It was a large cave that could sit almost a thousand badgers. One badger from each camp within a ten-mile radius was in attendance. Tonight, nine hundred and eighty-nine badgers arrived for the meeting, including Treeshoot, Autumn, and the ten rabbits. The aroma of the mulberry tree roots and petrichor wafted through the cave which made everyone relaxed yet alert.

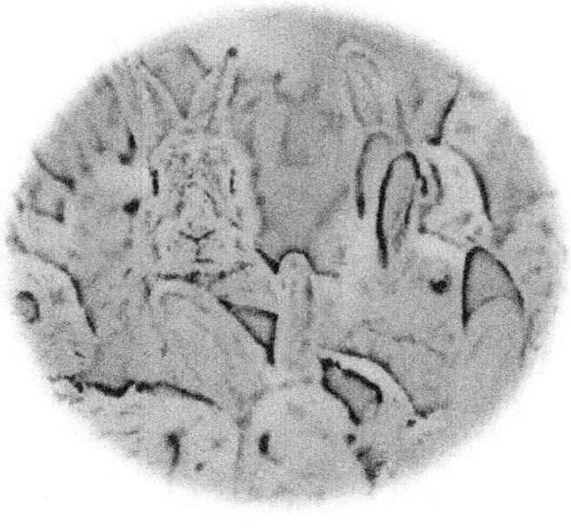

"Wow," said all the rabbits when they first entered the mud cave.

The badgers called it the Mulberry Cave because there was one of those beautiful trees above it. The captains sat behind the other rabbits. It was a protection pact which the rabbits did in unusual situations just like this one. Harper stood on the main stage and had a microphone in front of him.

"My dear badgers and welcome honorary guests, the rabbits," said Harper as he faced the crowd.

The rabbits sat in front of the stage so they could listen intently.

"We have found ourselves in this unexpected position. Our friends disappeared last night whilst trying to help us find more food. It seems that Thoric knew this was going to happen and has called on Cosimo to meet us here," said Harper.

Anyone could hear a pin drop; the atmosphere was electric.

"Cosimo, who is a white rabbit, Thoric, and the welcomed ten rabbits, will go to the Oakash Water Diggers tunnels and re-dig through them. This mission should enable our group to travel to the Milky Way," said Harper.

A huge grumble came over Mulberry Cave. Tens of badgers fainted, others could not speak, and hundreds of badgers stood on their hind legs and were asking Oscar and Harper questions.

“CALM!” shouted Oscar. “This is no time for panic or disorder,” he continued.

The loud rumbling of badgers subsided.

“Yes, I can understand why you are confused and scared. It appears that a Roman legend has come to life. Both Juno and Jupiter are in the Milky Way, looking for their grown son Hercules; and Thoric who has been our friend for four centuries is originally from a famous masterpiece, for those of you who do not know,” Oscar said.

“What?!” said the badgers and rabbits in unison.

“How do you know this?” shouted one of the badgers.

“Thoric met Cosimo at Burlington’s Ace-Portal today and he informed our friend. Please, no questions,” Oscar said.

"No, I meant how is Thoric from a painting. How is it possible that Hercules is alive and...?" shouted one of the badgers. Thoric explained the history of the painting and what had happened centuries ago.

By now it was 9 pm in England and the rabbits felt very tired.

"Tomorrow our rabbit friends - Captain Marlow, Captain Maplelog, Captain Lincoln, Patchy, Hopper, Harlequinn, Blazing Star, Little Bobbin, Rexus, and Laurel Tulipa; and Thoric, along with Cosimo will go to the Milky Way. Our Oakash Water diggers need our help. Come forward my dear rabbits and be counted for," said Harper.

All ten rabbits hesitantly walked toward the stage and sat on either side of Harper and Oscar. As Oscar continued speaking about Cosimo and Thoric, Little Bobbin turned to Captain Maplelog and said in a hushed voice "Oh my God!"

"What is it?" asked Laurel.

"The white rabbit is here!" replied Little Bobbin.

Before anyone could look around for Cosimo, he had run to the stage and was standing on a high bench that sat a metre away from Oscar and Harper.

"Welcome dear Cosimo," said Oscar and Harper. Oscar and Harper looked at each other in confusion. 'How had Cosimo known where they were?!' they thought.

"Cosimo is here," Autumn said in an elated voice. Her heart rate increased, and she was feeling more optimistic about saving their planet.

"Ah thanks to you Oscar and Harper," said Cosimo.

"How do you know our names?" asked Oscar.

"I know all animal names, I am Cosimo. I can see into the future. But I do not know if we can save the Oakash Water Diggers or the planets," answered the white rabbit. His English was exceptionally good.

"The rabbits are very strong, and I am sorry to say, faster at digging than badgers but I think we can all agree on this," all the animals started laughing because this was a known fact in the animal kingdom. "Rabbits can get up to speeds of 40 km per hour, whereas badgers can go as fast as 19 km per hour, therefore we have asked out Burlington friends to dig for us so they can get to the portal quicker. They need to recreate the tunnels to open the portals which will take us to the Milky Way. Hercules must come out of hiding inside UY Scuti and use his strength to pull the stars out of the ring of gravity. He must destroy black holes; Antares formed a new hole today, and we have less time than I thought before," said Cosimo. "We must gain the trust of Juno, Hercules, and Jupiter. Hercules has been learning to paint so he can recreate Tintoretto's painting because he wants to go home. He is trying to go back in time to save Tintoretto's painting from being put under a magical spell. He used his supernatural powers to transport two human artists from a London gallery to the planet and is forcing them to paint. Yes, there are humans on UY Scuti now, scared and confused. We must save them too. The rabbits will convince Hercules to help us," Cosimo took a deep breath and blurted out "Harper has told you who is leaving on this quest... we shall be called 'The Galaxy Travellers'... Tomorrow, we leave at sunrise!"

CHAPTER 13

The Milky Way Portal

Saturday morning, 28th March.

The weather had improved since the Oakash Water Diggers had left to create a passage to the berries. At 11 Celsius, 6.36 am, the ten rabbits prepared themselves for the quest ahead by filling up with seeds and British water, which was as fresh as a daisy. The water flood that the Oakash Water Diggers created, travelled down the nearest road to a farmer's cabbage patch. The local farmers had fixed the flood which made it easier for the Galaxy Travellers to cross the road. The disgruntled humans had no idea why there were holes in the canals and who had created this. Four farmers saw the bird and eleven rabbits all moving in the same direction which left perplexed expressions on their faces.
"What on God's Earth am I seeing?" asked an old father to his son.

"I cannot believe my eyes. I have never seen rabbits and birds together like this. And that white rabbit, how strange he seems," the farmer's son responded.

Cosimo found the entrances of the four tunnels and stood on the hill so he could address all the rabbits. He assigned all the rabbits travel buddies. Captain Marlow would go with Patchy and Harlequinn. Captain Maplelog would go with Hopper and Rexus. Captain Lincoln would travel with Blazing Star and Little Bobbin. Laurel would dig with Cosimo and Thoric. Laurel was the most excited because she got to travel with the oldest animals on planet earth."We shall travel through the tunnels as I have commanded. We shall dig as fast as you have ever dug before. Do not stop and eat any food, we will eat on the other side. You have great digging skills so use your paws wisely if there are obstructions on the way. The Milky Way's atmosphere is very alike to ours but the air is different. There is much unrest there, but we focus on our mission. Thoric cannot run fast so she will hold onto my scut to make this journey quicker. Once you arrive on the other side you will land on clouds. You must wait for everyone when you land on the ground. Understood?" Cosimo asked.

"Understood," replied all the rabbits who now felt

like sergeants.

"We start at these entrances, where the mud is still slightly wet from the canal outflow You will not come across any pools of water large enough to suffocate you as the farmers closed the leaks. Let us go now!" Cosimo said as he pointed to the four holes which had shrunk due to the river water.

The captains and the white rabbit all entered the tunnels first. They could smell the badgers who'd been there even though two nights had passed. The rabbits took little lamps which the badgers had given them the night before. The lamps sat on the traveller's backs and illuminated the passage ahead. The light made the journey more bearable for the rabbits because it gave them a shade of comfort in this unknown territory. The rabbits began digging very fast, faster than they had ever dug before.

"Do you see anything yet?" yelled out Laurel to Cosimo. She need not have yelled as sound travelled loudly underground despite there being less oxygen.

"We will be there very soon. I can see pink light ahead. Grab onto Thoric's feet as we come out," replied Cosimo.

Just as Cosimo finished speaking, they were at the exit and falling downwards on thick clouds. Laurel turned to the left, and she could see all the other rabbits sitting on their bottoms and looking around them in complete awe. She was so grateful that they had not fallen and were not climbing down another oak tree. Little Bobbin saw Laurel's cloud and waved at them. It took almost ten minutes before the adventurers reached the ground. Thoric flew around excitedly as she spotted the badgers. "I see the Oakash Water Diggers," yelled out Thoric as she flew down the hundred metres or so.

The clouds got in the way of the rabbit's view so they could not see where Thoric had flown. Then, the clouds parted, and they could smell lilies everywhere and see bushes with berries for hundreds of miles.

"There is Thoric," pointed Harlequinn towards the north of their descent.

Within a few minutes, all rabbits had landed safely on the ground. Cosimo instructed the rabbits to stay put while Thoric located the Oakash Digger's.

“I see Thoric,” shouted Little Bobbin in excitement.

“Good spotting my friends. Let us go towards her,” said Cosimo. The white rabbit stood on his hind legs so that he could locate the smell of the badgers.

“This is the badger’s path… let us follow that,” he said. Cosimo began running, followed by the others. Little did they know, except the white rabbit, that Autumn and Treeshoot had followed them and were descending on the clouds behind them. As the rabbits began running towards Thoric, they stopped once they heard footsteps behind them. Cosimo stood up on his hind legs and saw Treeshoot and Autumn running fifty metres behind.

“It is okay bunnies, our badger friends who welcomed you to the badger community, Autumn, and Treeshoot, have joined us. They informed their friend and came without the permission of Oscar or Harper. Autumn knows Thoric, they are old friends. She is very worried about Santiago and wishes more than anything to know that he is alive and well.”

"Oh, this is fantastic, she is exceedingly kind," said Little Bobbin.

"Let's wait for them," said Cosimo. The captains agreed.

As Autumn and Treeshoot caught up with the rabbits, a look of surprise came over them. Had the rabbits heard them coming all along?

"We just heard your footsteps now, but I knew you would join the Galaxy Travellers," said Cosimo.

"Will we be in trouble when we get back?" asked Treeshoot nervously. He was not one for disobeying orders and he was extremely uncomfortable about leaving Oakash without informing his leaders, but he wanted to help his best friend, Autumn. Autumn had persuaded him to go but Treeshoot did not need much persuading. His fear for his friend's disappearance and feelings of guilt that he had not attended the counsel meeting outweighed his code of disobedience. Autumn's fears over Santiago's wellbeing quickly ended because he came running over to her and they embraced.

"No, *squawk* you, brave warriors. And clever, yes. Good you came," replied Thoric.

The Oakash Water Diggers were shocked when they saw the eleven rabbits and two badgers approaching. Thoric had already flown towards them and told the Oakash Water Diggers that the rabbits had come to help them, and they are friends now. The badgers and rabbits rubbed noses together and would now recognise each other's scent. This was important, because should any of the animals get lost, one of them could trace the missing creature with their recorded scent.

Bonobos ordered the badgers to each take out a pawful of berries from their backpacks and give them to the new arrivals. Thoric was already eating berries which had changed from turquoise, red to a luminous yellow colour. She was incredibly happy and started squawking loudly.

"Quieter Thoric, you make too much noise," demanded Cosimo.

“We do not fear the land people here although they have strange features,” said Agent Sol.

“They gave us this rock and we believe that it will take us to the UY Scuti star where Hercules may be hiding. How strange we must sound to you,” said Llama staring at the crystal. The crystal was very rare, a mix of crystal with elements of stone particles.

“Not strange to me dear Llama, Hercules is hiding in the red supergiant star.” Cosimo went on to explain everything to the Oakash Water Diggers.

“OH!” said the original Water Oakash Diggers. None of them believed the Indigenous women's drawing of the humans in the UY Scuti. They were grateful that the kind woman had been so honest with them. Everything was starting to make sense now to the badgers from the Oakash Water Diggers who had been questioning what was happening to the stars and why they moved.

“Now we know what has occurred here and I truly feel compelled to help,” said Santiago.

“They have three eyes,” said Tanto whilst looking at Cosimo. “Why is this?” he asked.

“Their third eye is a prophecy eye. They can see the

future, too, like me. Their cosmic eye gives them the ability to time-travel too," Cosimo answered.

The pact had become united on this mission and there was no turning away from the dangers that lay ahead.

"Up there, look, the four angels are coming towards us," blurted Tanto.

"What do they want from us? We saw them yesterday and one of the angels held a torch for Juno which tells us that they are of the divine sort," asked Figs.

"They are coming to help us. Or maybe they will try to stop us from moving away from here," replied Tanto who was suspicious of the angels.

"They come to help. They each have a tool that can assist us. See, one angel has a bow and arrow which can make anyone fall in love with oneself or another. Another angel has the torch to light the way. One of the angels has a chain that should hold Hercules's hands together if he starts to misbehave; he would put Hercules's hands in a chain. The fourth angel has a net which we will need to use when we first meet Hercules to stop him from flying away from us," said Cosimo. Cosimo was like a talking encyclopaedia.

"How do you know this?" asked Figs.

"He gift of foresight *squawk*," replied Thoric who was chirpier since arriving on this planet.

"We never heard of a rabbit that can see into the future. Unusual gift. Excuse me Cosimo but which camp do you come from?" asked Captain Maplelog.

"Me, not from the camp, I come from a masterpiece 'The Madonna and her Rabbit' painted in 1530 by the renowned artist Titian. I came out of the painting the same day as Thoric, but I came through the canvas before my friend, so I went to Tintoretto's art studio to look for Thoric because I knew she would also come out of the painting. Tintoretto heard me when I was in the kitchen so I escaped back out before he could see me. Thoric and I became great friends on that day," said Cosimo with joy.

"So much we do not know," said Winstone.

"We think we know much about our history but there is more to learn. We must never stop learning," said Sparrowsky.

"Agreed Sparrowsky. Life is full of opportunities to gain experience and learn," Winstone affirmed to Sparrowsky.

The four angels had arrived and were hovering above the animals. They could not speak but were waving their gifts around to communicate with the animals.

"They say that Juno has sent them to help us," said Cosimo to ease the confusion among the travellers. "They say we must go now because the black hole by UY Scuti is so close to sucking it in and we will never be able to save the earth or the Milky Way from destruction. They say the newest black hole is dangerously close to pulling the entire Scorpius constellation to its gravitational field," he continued.

The four angels created a circle formation above the animals, and the travellers stood in a circle underneath them, whilst Thoric stood on the ground in the centre. Winstone took the crystal out of his backpack and saw that it was vibrating and little specks of dust of crystal rotated around it. Winstone was shocked and threw it up in the air but quickly caught the rock before it could crash onto the ground. He passed the rock to Cosimo who looked at it and seemed to fall into the stone. The white rabbit fell against the glowing berry bush and his eyes became withdrawn, like he was oscillating between sleep and wakefulness. The magnetic energy of the crystal dust had drawn Cosimo into its power of transportation which only divine creatures could feel.

"Wake up!" said Thoric.

"Yes, I just got lost in the stars of the crystal," said Cosimo. He felt weak for a second, somehow the rock had pulled him in, but he regained his composure. Thankfully he was pulled out of the rocks magnetic field otherwise he may have been transported into it.

"The fate of the constellations will reveal their true nature to us," Sparrowsky said, smiling at Cosimo.

Cosimo wondered if Sparrowsky had the gift of prophecy too. Cosimo then looked around him and thought there were too many of them to go to UY Scuti together, and the crystal stone might not have the strength to take them all. So, he decided that three rabbits and five badgers would stay behind.

"Tanto, Figs, Patchy, Captain Maplelog, Rexus, Treeshoot, Autumn, and Harlequinn- you eight shall remain here and keep the portal open so we may return safely back to earth! Should anything happen to us, you can get help from the indigenous people on this planet," ordered Cosimo.

The rabbits and badgers looked stunned. 'Why would Cosimo not let them join the group?' thought the remaining animals to themselves.

"Do not feel upset my dear friends. We cannot all go together; the crystal does not possess the power for so many of us to cosmic travel."

"I will see you soon my dear," Santiago said to Autumn as they embraced. She hardly spent more than twenty minutes with Santiago, and they were being separated again.

"I will look after them," said Captain Maplelog with renewed confidence. He was given the chance to protect these animals, which was something he enjoyed doing. "We shall see you upon your return, my fellow Galaxy Travellers. Make haste and may the stars shine upon you with streaks of luck," he continued.

Cosimo's group separated from Captain Maplelog's group so the remaining team would not accidentally be drawn into the power of the crystal rock. Cosimo held the crystal with his front left foot and rubbed it with his right front foot. The earth started to rumble underneath them. A crack began to form under their feet. Thoric flew up from the reverberations but remained below the angels. Then a purple and orange/red wind enveloped them all and created a whooshing vortex. As the vortex powered to 1000 km per hour, the animals lifted into the air. They were pulled into the whirlwind which was making their heads spin. The animal's little heads began to feel drowsy. They were spinning inside the vortex but at a much slower speed.

The travellers could see more of the planet from this height. There were thousands of lilies for thousands of miles around them. Makeshift homes with rivers everywhere. Hundreds of the homes were camouflaged behind bushes or strange-looking trees. Berries were everywhere.

The tree roots came out of the earth and mushrooms rested on them. The roots were waving the mushrooms around which released small microorganisms of psilocybin into the air. The grounded animals began to see the constellation of stars differently. The colours were more vivid, and tens of the constellations seemed to yawn like they were waking up after centuries of deep slumber.

Then the dark-haired inhabitants came out of their homes and began jumping up and down whilst waving their hands in the shape of the infinity symbol. In between their hands was their third eye which had moved from their forehead. They were singing songs that none of the animals or bird had ever heard of. The songs sounded old, older than the big bang: and the music was like it was created by the stars themselves, a very electric and crystal type of sound.

Juno came from behind one of the stars, flew towards them, and smiled. Then she saw Jupiter who was heading toward the animals, and she became concerned because of his temper, so she quickly turned around and held Jupiter back. One of the angels sent one of his nets which captured Jupiter and stopped him from sabotaging the quest of the Galaxy Travellers. Jupiter was enraged but quickly silenced when the angel of love shot his bow at him. He fell into a sleep in the sky, and to avoid any unpleasant injuries, the angels and Juno gently brought his body down to the Planet of the Lilies. Holding their breath, the angels quickly flew upwards and caught up with the animals in the vortex whilst Juno remained with her partner. The badgers and rabbits all looked at each other in astonishment. Certainly, for the badgers and rabbits, this was not something that they had ever seen on any screen. This was real life.

CHAPTER 14

UY Scuti

Saturday, late morning.

The vortex travelled past millions of spectacular stars and the animals even saw the black hole, well not the actual black hole because it is impossible to see one without being pulled into it. No, what they saw was old stardust spinning almost 1/2 a million kilometres per hour and passing into an abyss. Once the stardust got to the inner regions of the dark hole, it just seemed to disappear.

Millions of stars shone so brightly, and their light beamed toward planet earth and the moon. The rock members were in absolute awe of the marvellous spectacle surrounding them. The Galaxy Travellers went past the Eagle Nebula, which astounded Thoric. They saw the Omega Nebula, the Sagittarius Star Cloud, and many more constellations until they reached one of the biggest stars, the magnificent UY Scuti. This humungous star was a deep red colour, and almost seventeen hundred times bigger than the sun. No wonder Jupiter could not find Hercules. This star was very bright and hot, but the vortex protected them from the dangerous brightness and heat of the twinkling old dust. The whirlwind took them inside the star.

“For the first time... I’m very scared,” said Little Bobbin.

“Me too, Little Bobbin,” said his best friend. The rabbits and badgers huddled closer together.

Cosimo and Thoric were not scared but they were concerned.

‘Will they survive this?’ Cosimo was pondering to himself. Storms were raging everywhere. Normally, there would be no breathable air on these stars, but Jupiter had struck lightning with thunderstorms in this galaxy, creating an atmosphere. Red dust balls were circling the star, which was whooshing past them at lightning speed. They could see humongous mountains, sometimes on top of other enormous mountains. There were stars inside UY Scuti, which, along with the red lava lakes, made things more visible on this planet. Parts of the star were in complete darkness, while other areas were visible.

The Galaxy Travellers could feel the intense heat from the thousands of lava lakes. The huge lakes were bigger than the size of South and North America put together. Strange bats in every shade of red and as big as a cat flew past them and into the lakes. They were feeding on tiny lava fishes. The vortex began to descend towards the north-west of the star. It was travelling sideways. There was so much dust, and when it hit another dust ball it disintegrated into small flames.

Llama and Sparrowsky saw it first. In the distance

stood a mountainous rock with a small light shining from inside one of the crevices, about five hundred metres up, with music coming from within. The crevice stood about one hundred metres up, and as the crew got closer, they could see lights blazing from fifty metres tall candles. The entrance was so huge that the new arrivals could see hundreds of candles standing erect and stuck to the floor with wax. The room was so vast that they could not see any endings to the cave. Behind the first ten candles, a smaller room on the left was also lit by candles but these were much smaller, about ten metres high. When the wax fell, it would sizzle as it touched the red dusty floor and burst into flames. The flames then turned into black smoky creatures that disappeared into the darkness of the cave. They could all hear classical music and Cosimo knew it was Hercules speaking from inside the room. Every time Hercules spoke, the music was drowned out because his voice was like a thunderous roar, and no human could speak like that. The beautiful angel who had the net was preparing to throw it at Hercules as the threat of his erratic behaviour drew closer to them.

The vortex began to reduce speed and was coming down, slowly to the ground. Eventually, they all landed safely, and the vortex disappeared around them into the black nothingness behind the candles. Suddenly, the group felt more vulnerable without the protective shield. To add to the eeriness of the place was a strange sound coming from above.

Winstone looked up and said, "Maybe bat, or other bird."

The angel with the torch flew up and illuminated the space above it. As he ascended higher, the light fell upon lizard-looking creatures on the walls. These lizards had five eyes the size of golf balls that glowed red, and a one-metre tail on their head that swayed when they moved. The creature had two sets of feet which were parallel to each other, and two sets of wings on either side of its body. The wings had black and red spots and an iridescent shimmer that almost looked green when they shuffled. They were attracted to the light of the torch angel.

The torch angel went to the closest lizard and spoke in its ear. The creature was hanging bizarrely off the thick mountainous wall, hanging on to it with its four feet at the opposite end of its head. It was speaking to the angel, making a sound like grasshoppers but at different pitches. Thousands of these strange beings came into the light shadow of the torch. They seemed upset. The angel came back and told the white rabbit that the lizards had been living in the star since it was first formed. They said that Hercules had been creating a huge amount of noise and was scaring them. Thousands of their kind had disappeared one month ago since Hercules had been hiding in their cave. They had not been able to leave for a long time and were growing very weary and tired of feeling trapped.

Trembling with fear, the badgers and rabbits looked scared with wide eyes, open mouths, and shivering bodies. Hercules had flown near the entrance of the room he was in; they saw his wavy hair and strangely-shaped body. He was speaking to the abducted humans and ordering them to mix the colours for the peacock from Tintoretto's painting: "That blue is much too dark, lighten it!" They could see bits of paint over his body, on the floor and walls; even the candles had splashes of paint over them.

Anticipating Hercules's next move, the angel with the net flew to the side of the entrance but remained hidden. The animals also stood behind the walls on both sides. Thoric was standing on Captain Marlow's head, while the white rabbit watched on the other side of the entrance. The opening was about five metres wide. Then they saw two humans who were the artists that Hercules had abducted from planet earth. They were standing by a rock that formed a shelf, and they were talking about which correct paint colours to use to complete the body of the peacock. You could hear their voices quivering and see their arms shaking.

Hercules was very unpredictable. He moved everywhere inside the paint room; sometimes he would even go out of sight and then return out of nowhere. He told the humans he was going to get them food from the Planet of the Lilies so the angel with the net quickly prepared his net. Cosimo knew that the animals waiting on the

Planet of the Lilies would be safe, even if Hercules did spot them. The angel drew his arms back and started circling the net around very quickly. Seizing their opportunity, the angels released their net and caught Hercules as he began to fly out of the chamber. In a huge rage, he threw his arms up and tried to release himself from the trap, but no mortal or immortal being could release themselves from an angel's net. Then the angel of love aimed his bow and arrow at Hercules and released it. It shot him in the heart, but it did not pierce his body. Instead, the bow disappeared, his whole body glowed a light pink and the bow had worked its magic on Hercules. The angel with the chain threw his attribute and it floated around Hercules's arms and feet until it wrapped them. Hercules then fell into a sleep and began to fall, but the angels caught him and lay him gently on the ground.

The humans watched everything unfold and dropped their paintbrushes on the ground. Cosimo hopped over to the humans and began explaining everything to them whilst the angels waited for Hercules to come out of his sleep. It did not take long before he woke up and tried to sit up, but the net weighed so much that he was unable to even move. "What is going on here?" Hercules asked.

"We need your help, Hercules," replied Thoric.

"But you are the eagle from the painting which I have been trying to recreate. I did not know you looked like that... no wonder my drawings never worked," Hercules said.

"You can draw your painting after you help us. We help you to restore the Origin of the Milky Way painting. But now, you must save this galaxy!" exclaimed Thoric. This was the first ever sentence where Thoric did not squawk. Thoric remembered the last time that she saw Hercules was when she was trying to escape the tornados in the painting. Thoric took a deep breath in and remembered the danger she felt when she saw herself separated from Hercules, and the others, and seeing him now made her feel safer.

"Why should I help you? I am helping myself. Long tired am I from living in this galaxy and I want to return home," said Hercules.

"I live on earth for almost five centuries. Cosimo too. We want to go home. But something dangerous is happening in the Milky Way. Can you not see what is happening *squawk*?" asked Thoric.

"I have noticed changes of colour in the sky but not put my attention to it. I thought my paintings were causing that. My incessant paint colouring was changing the colour of the space around me, but I badly perceived things," replied Hercules.

"Yes, you have misunderstood but I can understand why you did. Two black holes are trying to pull UY Scuti and Antares stars into their gravitational pull. Soon, there will be no Milky Way, no earth, no humans, no animals, no life whatsoever!" Bonobos exclaimed.

"What!?" Hercules shouted. His voice reverberated throughout the cave and echoed for ages. Hercules pondered on how busy he had been trying to recreate the Renaissance painting, that he had not acknowledged the changes occurring in the galaxy around him.

"Please help us," said Winstone in a quivering voice.

"But I did not know this. How did this happen?" Hercules asked.

"There are many reasons for this," Cosimo said as

he run towards them.

“The white rabbit?” Hercules asked.

“Yes, I am from Titian’s painting, I am called Cosimo,” he replied.

“I cannot believe my eyes. First, I see Thoric, and now I see the white rabbit. This is like a strange dream…” he rubbed his eyes, “I thought it was a myth that you had escaped Titian’s painting, but now I see the legend is true. How did you escape?!” Hercules asked with his natural authority.

Every time Hercules spoke, the animals could feel his voice vibrate in their bodies. He was frightening but at the same time, his strength which could be felt from the energy he emitted, was reassuring.

“Since Tintoretto’s painting was the most powerful in the Renaissance, and it was about the creation of the Milky Way, the paints began to create this reality. Titian and many other artists were supreme painters, but Tintoretto had spent many years on his canvas, and it accumulated a lot of energy. Now, you must use all your strength to pull the stars out of the black hole’s orbit. Life will end if you do not help us,” Cosimo answered.

"Once you do this, we can help you to restore the original masterpiece, once known as the Nursing of 'Hercules'. Will you help us?" the white rabbit asked. He looked into Hercules's eyes and hoped that he would see how Tintoretto's painting was originally drawn with Hercules as the main story.

"Yes, you help us, we help you, and you help us to help you," Thoric squawked.

Hercules nodded his head and looked at all the animals, the eagle, and the white rabbit. "Dear friends, I am yours now and a friend." He had calmed down.
"How are so many earthly animals here?" he asked. The angels took the net and chains of Hercules. Laurel went on to explain the last few day's activities. Then, Hercules stood up very slowly and held his head in his hands because he was feeling dizzy. The animals were scared and stood up on their hind legs, as if ready to do battle.

"Do not worry my friends, Hercules is not a bad immortal. I trust him. He has a dizzy head from the love bow," reassured Cosimo. But the animals were still quite timid.

The humans heard everything, and they had to lean against each other to not fall over. They were feeling very overwhelmed.

“How do we get back to earth?” asked the female. She was very noticeable and not because of her short brunette hair and sparkling blue eyes, but because her glasses moved quickly around her nose and forehead from the fear inside her. Her name was Camilla.

“We will go back through the tunnels on the Planet of the Lilies. And then we will take you home in our cabins,” answered Agent Sol. “We want to go back home. I miss my family. Oh, and by the way, my name is Agent Sol, nice to meet you,” he said.

Camilla nervously smiled back but could not speak because she was in shock that animals were speaking to her.

“Her name is Camilla… she is very scared like me. We have not even spoken to each other all week about our current experience since we first arrived here which happened without our consent… I do wonder what my family must be thinking of me right now,” John filled in and said what Camilla wanted to say. “My name is John…” he finished saying in a quivering voice.
“How will they fit through the tunnels?” asked Hopper.

"An Ace-Portal is being created by the local people for your return, well, not exactly an Ace-Portal cabin like the badgers, but a tree cabin. They are wise people and have strong trees which can move people under the earth's crust faster and safely. They will open the tree portal for you once we return to the Planet of the Lilies," Cosimo answered.

Just as Little Bobbin was about to speak, they heard something strange coming from the west of the cave.

"Hopper, can you and Captain Marlow go and see what that is about?" asked Cosimo. Hopper was an amazingly fast runner and had to stop to allow the captain to catch up. The two humans seemed to relax more.

"How will we get there or even leave this star?" asked Laurel.

"I gained supernatural powers when I drank from Juno's breast. I can carry you all and protect you from the heat of this star," replied Hercules.

"But how can you carry us all with you?" asked Blazing Star and Santiago at the same time. Both animals looked at each other and slightly giggled.

"I will cut a large piece of rock and sit you all

on it. Then I will place an energy field around everyone and pull you myself to the place of lilies. A long time has my strength been tested," Hercules responded.

"Excuse me, dear friend. My name is Little Bobbin from the Maple Tree in Burlington. The rabbits and the badgers came together yesterday for the first time since the great disaster, because of what is happening to this star system. And now we have made peace with each other. You really can trust us."

Hercules looked at the rabbit as he tied his hair back. Surprisingly, Hercules smiled and chuckled. He enjoyed how much these animals spoke. Hopper and Captain Marlow came running back. They were out of breath, and what they were saying made no sense.

"BIG, DRAGON, coming!!" yelled Hopper.

"Its legs are taller than a mountain. Its claws are everywhere on its body. And it has many eyes, many scarlet eyes!" said Captain Marlow.

Everyone could hear loud thumps echoing from the back vastness of the cave. The hairs on the animal's body stood up and their eyes dilated. The animals were terrified.

Hercules quickly flew off into the darkness, beyond the candles, and returned a few minutes afterwards with a rock that would seat all the animals, humans, and birds. He was working quickly because this dragon could kill anyone with his breath, and they did not have very much time left. Without any instruction, the Galaxy Travellers and humans ran onto the rock and sat down. Hercules flew above the rock and waved his arms, which created a protective energy field around it.

"He works very fast," said John. He was 54 years old, tall, wore glasses, and had black curly hair with chestnut brown eyes. Both humans explained they had been working at The Courtauld Gallery in London, repairing Renaissance masterpieces when Hercules kidnapped them late one evening. John explained that they both fainted and do not remember how they got to this star. Now, all the animals understood why Hercules had chosen them.

Hercules lifted the rock with his left hand and his right arm lay by his side.

"He is very strong'" said Laurel aloud.

As Hercules carried the rock outside of the crevice, they could see the fiery lava spewing up huge fire springs about one thousand feet into the air. Then another fire spring flew up into the air near the moving rock. All of a sudden, there was a tornado above them which had lightning and thunder inside it. It formed a connection with the lake and created a lava whirlwind. Within the whirlwind were bizarre-looking fishes that seemed to be growing wings and trying to escape the vortex but could not, much like Thoric's experience in the masterpiece when she tried to pull herself out of the strong whirlwind which had trapped her.

Everyone could hear the crackling sounds of the

heat emerging from the huge volcanoes. The volcanoes were four times the size of Mount Everest. Hercules quickly pushed the rock away from the lava whirlwind and escaped the deathly power of the fire springs. He lifted the rock higher and higher until they were flying past the red-hot dust clouds, on the surface of this enormous star. Hercules was stunned when they came out of UY Scuti because the galaxy had changed since he had been collaborating with the humans. The animals started to feel better once they left the star. It was too dramatic for their liking. The humans also seemed more relieved once they were out of the star.

Hercules stopped pushing the rock and faced what he believed was the site of the black hole. He did not need anyone to tell him where to look because he could use his extrasensory skills. He left the rock floating in the darkness of space, but close to the Eagle Nebula. The angels came out of the energy field and began scanning for the black hole by the star.

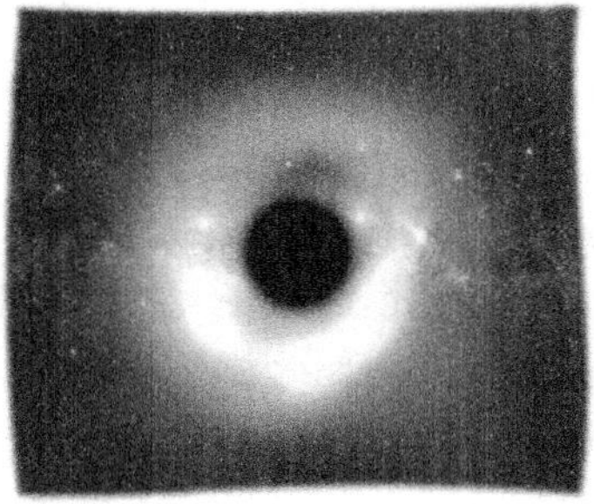

Hearing a curious sound, Hercules saw Jupiter and Juno fly towards him. Hercules was roaring with anger at his father but quickly calmed down when Juno embraced him. She had a healing touch in her fingertips which had always helped to relax the turbulent Hercules. Still a little agitated but with a clear mind, Hercules explained to his father and Jupiter what the new arrivals had informed him.

"We must help you, son," Juno said as she stared at Jupiter. Juno had accepted Hercules as her son centuries ago. Jupiter was still angry that the angels had bewitched him with their tools, but just as he was becoming enraged again, and lightning was forming around his body, he heard Thoric and then wept at recognition of the great bird from the painting.

For the first time in years, Jupiter felt happy. Seeing

Thoric was like being at home again, in a painting where he felt at peace. The black eagle reminded him of the mythological stories surrounding him and his eagle, the messenger. 'Is this Thoric my messenger?' Jupiter asked himself. Jupiter embraced Thoric and the bird squawked in joy. The star had never heard joy like this before.

Jupiter offered his power of lightning and thunderstorm. "I shall help thee. We can forge our powers together and push that black hole to oblivion."

Hercules nodded in agreement to his father. Juno went ahead and went feeling for the start of the black hole. Although she could hear the roaring silence of the dark vortex, nobody had seen it.

"I hear it, it is much stronger here," shouted Juno. The angels came to Juno and held out their hands; they could also feel the energy vibration of strong gravity. Hercules and Jupiter hovered over Juno and the angels.

"This black hole is enormous but weak in power. I shall create anti-gravity matter and throw it in," shouted Hercules.

"How is that possible?" asked Winstone.

"But Hercules has supernatural powers, and he can create anything he wants to" responded Blazing Star... "we heard him say that he gained these powers in this galaxy," she continued.

"What is anti-gravity?" asked Hopper.

"It's not been seen with the naked eye, but scientists claim it exists. I need more time to explain what it is," replied Bonobos. Bonobos loved science documentaries and started to look forward to teaching the animals about this fascinating topic.

The animals and the bird gazed at the Renaissance figures as they were conjuring their strength. As Hercules rotated his arms rapidly, a cyclone of millions of atoms began to spin so quickly that the atoms became one large ball of force. Hercules lifted this energy sphere and threw it towards the black hole. Everyone was anxious because what if Hercules missed the black hole, it could have devastating effects on the Milky Way. Everyone held their breath. Then, the energy ball magically disappeared. The black hole started to make further noise and the outside of it became visible because you could see hot matter surrounding it, which looked like blazing red flames. Stardust particles came out but they did not hurt anyone.

As the black chasm was disintegrating, it appeared and then disappeared, so the space behind it was visible when the blackness was gone, and then disappeared when the dark hole reappeared. The abyss had finally disintegrated into nothingness. One could sense the change in the air, there was a peacefulness amongst the stars nearby. They seemed quiet now, whereas before they emitted a sound of melancholy.

Then Cosimo saw a glimpse of Hercules. Juno, Jupiter, and the angels trying unsuccessfully to destroy the black hole. It was a thousand times harder to demolish because it was engaged with Antares's gravitational field from the Scorpius constellation.

"Hooray, hooray to Hercules," the animals were shouting.

The angels smiled and so did Juno and Jupiter. Hercules combed his hair back with his fingers and smiled. He was a picture of perfection.

"We must not get too excited," shouted Cosimo.

"My friend Hercules, the biggest challenge is the

Antares black hole *squawk*," said Thoric.

"How will Hercules and his family destroy that one?" asked Llama.

"I still cannot see it... my vision beyond this moment is no longer," replied Cosimo. Cosimo did not want to share what he had just foreseen.

"We must think of the best outcome, for all I can think of is going back home," said Hopper.

Hercules came over to the rock and said "Next black hole is too dangerous for your mortal souls. I shall return once we have obliterated it!"

The earthly animals could not speak; they were still in awe of this formidable being who was merciful and supporting their quest. Thoric and Cosimo were less impressed for they were from that era of tragedy folk tales.

"Will you stay with us?" Captain Marlow asked Thoric and Cosimo.

"Yes, we *squawk* have no choice but to remain," responded Thoric.

"We wait for your return, dear friends," said Captain Lincoln. Captain Lincoln was also desperately missing home; in fact, all the earthly animals were. Sparrowsky and Agent Sol both locked eyes and you could see their wishes in their eyes - the smoky wood fires burning from their homes, the sweet smell of berries, the hot drinks, and the comfort of their homes. The animals started to feel very homesick.

CHAPTER 15

Antares

Saturday afternoon.

Suspecting the worst, Hercules, Juno, Jupiter, and the four angels waved at all the animals sitting on the rock and flew with their superpowers towards Antares. They all seemed calm and prepared to embark on their quest to destroy the largest black hole. It was several hundreds of miles away, but these unearthly beings could fly at turbo speed.

"Son, will you speak to me now?" asked Jupiter.

"Not the time to discuss any issues of concern father," Hercules replied.

"Fine son, and yes, it's best to not stray our minds from the work ahead," Jupiter said.

As they scanned the horizon, the seraphs saw it was very dark in parts of space so the angel of the torch held out its lantern to illuminate the way ahead. The beautiful stars and their colours made them all feel stronger. As they all approached Antares, they could feel vibrational energy coming from the dark vortex. All they could hear was a deep, deafening silence. Antares was turning red like a star does when it is ready to supernova.

Jupiter began striking lightning towards the area of the black hole. After repeating this a hundred times, they now knew where the borders of the black hole were. The angel who held the bow and arrow released his shot into the black hole. The torch angel lit the tip of the arrow so they could see it through the darkness of the black vacuum. The angels enjoyed watching how the bow with light at its tip spun around in circles before, eventually, reaching the point of singularity where every object is crushed and nothing could ever come back. The force of energy was tremendous around them. They all had to be careful not to enter the realm of the black hole's gravitational pull because if they were pulled in, there was no possibility that they could come back out. No immortal being with supernatural powers had the strength or wisdom to bring anything out of the gravity force.

Juno, Hercules, the four angels together, and

Jupiter all flew to separate parts of the black hole. They flew very carefully by sensing the gravity pull. Every time they felt too close to it, they would move further away. Eventually, they were all at the north, south, east, and west positions of the black abyss. Hercules, Juno, and Jupiter began chanting Renaissance poetry of Roman history, and loudly. This was what they had to do to gather their strengths:

> Oh, lead us to our pearly earth,
> We shall repaint the starry birth,
> Glorious and almighty you shine,
> But your planet is different from thine,
> The sound of swooshing water lava,
> Propel thoughts of seeing the dhava,
> Take us far from this black space,
> I promise to return with heavenly grace.

Hercules punched the outer region of the black hole with his right fist. This caused the hole to wobble and change shape. Suddenly, the two peacocks and the red crab from the Origin of the

Milky Way painting came out of the black hole and flew out.

"Oh, my goodness!" shouted Jupiter loudly.

The peacocks and crab looked stunned. 'Where had they been?' they all thought. 'Maybe this is a good omen' thought Hercules to himself. The angels spoke to the crab and peacocks and instructed them to look for the rock with the Galaxy Travellers, and two humans on it by UY Scuti. The crab held onto the peacocks and both flew in the direction of UY Scuti.

'The earthly beings will be even more stunned once they meet them,' thought Juno. Jupiter kept moving around the border of the black hole and striking lightning into the centre of it. The lightning was gigantic, and an enormous brightness and powerful rumble of thunder followed. Juno was chanting to protect all life. Her song entered the black abyss, and its pure sound penetrated through the hole. Suddenly, the deep hollow erupted from within, like a supernova. Its powerful energy catapulted them all backwards. Had the black hole grown bigger?

The Rock

The powerful energy of the backlash from the black abyss had reached the rock with the animals on it and pushed it back into UY Scuti The animals and humans almost lost their footing and had to hold onto the rock very tightly otherwise they could fall into one of the boiling lakes and perish.

“This is not good,” said Santiago.

“We might not be so well protected here without Hercules and the angels,” said Little Bobbin.

“We’ll have to hope the lava lakes or birds don’t attack us,” Sparrowsky added.

“What’s happened Cosimo?!” asked Agent Sol.

“The power of the black hole has created strong energy which has reached us here. They are working hard to destroy the black hole. May the figures of our constellations look after them,” Cosimo said as he closed his eyes.

The star became very raucous; hotter temperatures changed every metre, birds flew wildly, little strange fish jumped out of the lakes, hot lava geysers, and loud thunderous lightning grew stronger. The peacocks and crab entered the UY Scuti planet and joined the others on the rock. They were safer in the energy field. All the animals stood back as the peacocks and crab descended towards them.

"I never thought I would see the day!" Little Bobbin said.

"I have never seen a peacock in real life, little alone two of them," said Llama.

"You can see peacocks in Kew Gardens," said Santiago.

"Where did they come from?!" asked Laurel to the animals.

"They came out of a wormhole as Hercules and his family were trying to destroy it," Cosimo replied.

"Have they destroyed it?" asked Captain Marlow.

"No," was all Cosimo could say. He could not tell now what was happening to the Antares' black chasm, but he was more optimistic now that the peacocks and crab had come out of it.

The crab started to walk towards Thoric and tried to claw her but the peacocks held it back. Thoric flew up as the crab approached and escaped its clutches. Hopper moved to the other side of the rock where the humans were sat; he was quite scared of these beings. Santiago and Llama joined Hopper because they were also feeling intimidated.

"LOOK!" Camilla shouted as she pointed upwards.

The constellations of Cassiopeia, Andromeda, Orion, Perseus, and many others morphed into three-dimensional shapes. They were ginormous and dazzling. The constellations metamorphosed together in the shape of an infinity and were swirling around. The infinity ring had images of the Galaxy Travellers. It was beautiful to watch. Within minutes, the constellations were travelling towards Antares.

"Never in my animal years have I seen anything like this. I did not even know constellations were alive!" exclaimed Cosimo.

“Are they going to help our friends?” asked Hopper.

“Yes,” smiled Cosimo.

The energy field of the large rock was getting weaker. ‘Bragh, bragh, bragh’ sounds came from behind the huge mountain where they had found Hercules. Over a hundred large birds with red beaks bigger than their bodies, dark scarlet wings, and green feet, flew past them. The birds could not see the animals because of the protective shield. As the birds flew past, they did a detour and flew back around the rock. They were picking up a faint smell and it was prey-like. But the shield prevented the birds from detecting any prey so they flew away from the rock and disappeared.

“Phew, that was close. If we had been caught, I am certain we would have been their supper," said Winstone.

“It would have been the end of us for certain. I just hope Hercules comes back soon,” Blazing Star added.

“Let us hope they have united in this and will take us to safety, away from this fiery place. Oh, home, sweet Badgercom home.” As Winstone said this, the animals relaxed and started rubbing each other's noses.

"My dear Maribel must be worried about me," said Captain Marlow.

"She is making your bed and has placed some lavender herbs by a hot pot so she can make you tea when you arrive," said Cosimo to Captain Marlow.

Captain Marlow felt warmth in his heart and began to fantasise about being able to tell Maribel about his quest.

"Look at us," whispered Blazing Star, "Our King and Queen would be so proud of us because we're united with the badgers," she continued.

"We never thought we would ever reunite," said Agent Sol smiling.

"It took a great catastrophe for us to reconcile our differences," said Little Bobbin.

"You must come to stay with us," Blazing Star said to the badgers.

"And you too, of course," she said to Thoric and Cosimo.

"Autumn always speaks highly of you both," said

Santiago to Thoric and Little Bobbin. Santiago began remembering when Autumn told him, in secret, years ago: "I remember when Thoric asked me if I would help sneak a captive rabbit into the cabin so he could join Burlington. A few of the other badgers saw this rabbit but they pretended not to see anything."

"How and when did you meet Thoric? Not many rabbits have met Thoric except the badgers," Llama asked Little Bobbin.

"We met two or so years ago..." responded Little Bobbin. He told the story of the other animals that he lived with and the difficulties getting out through the earth.

"Autumn told me about you. But I thought she was exaggerating so I just listened to her talk, and nodded my head," Santiago laughed.

"Me friendly bird. I friend with all. You're friends now *squawk*. Me happy," said Thoric to all the earthly animals.

"We have you to thank for this Thoric," said Blazing Star. "Cosimo, thanks to you, we came together," she continued saying.

"It is the best time to make new friends. A new moon tomorrow so you can celebrate with boundless joy if we survive this," Cosimo responded.

Cosimo noticed how all the animals looked a bit sad, so he said, "I am sure we will be home soon. We must have faith." The atmosphere improved again.

"I feel very happy we are all friends and our Rabbitdom has now included Badgercom. This is beautiful," he said. "We have an eternity to celebrate our friendship now," said Agent Sol.

"Hooray," said Camilla.

Even the pessimistic badgers were feeling more positive.

The animals on the rock went silent again. None of them noticed that the protective shield was diminishing, and very quickly.

Back to Antares

'Whooo... whooo' sounds came from the great void. It had shrunk to half its size. The immortals could sense the dark hole had grown weaker in strength and was out of reach of the large star. But they could not allow the black hole to continue because it might grow again, or merge with another black abyss that would double its strength and destroy everything within the galaxy.

Astonishingly, the black hole which had shrunk now tripled in size. Their bodies were all catapulted further away from the dark source but they scrambled back to the outer regions of the abyss with every ounce of their energy. The catapult was the equivalent of one-hundred and fifty per cent efficiency, far greater power than any energy created from a supernova. The divine beings were feeling depleted and nervous. They were further deflated as they saw the black area had grown and blocked the outline of the constellation Scorpius which it is a part of. Antares is the beating heart of the Scorpius constellation and the black abyss needed to be annihilated otherwise the entire cluster would forever disappear inside it and start the death of the Milky Way.

Juno unexpectedly realised that parts of the Scorpion cluster had been sucked into the event horizon and then jetted out of the black hole at the same moment that they were pushed away, much to her delight. Juno's insight helped her to regain her full strength and she swiftly sent sounds of musical light that were heard loudly inside the point of singularity, which caused it to shrink one-tenth smaller. Shrinking the dark matter was enough to stop the mouth of it from touching Scorpius.

"Son, Jupiter, my angels, you must continue to destroy this," Juno shouted above the loud sounds. Hercules took a deep breath and continued applying powerful pressure. But the great dark void had grown stronger, and their work against it was insignificant. As their hope started to dwindle, the constellations arrived. They appeared to walk through the dark space like humans and illuminate the path in front of them. Hercules, angels, Juno, and Jupiter were pleased to see them because they knew that the constellations were part of the galaxies' history where time began, and where life was created after the big bang. The stars were huge yet moved with magnificent ease, emitting strong energy.

Jupiter wondered if his constellation was amongst them, but he could not see through all the illuminated stars. The angels were flying around the black hole, sending their special talents to it. Juno developed magical strengths and began sending bright, luminous light, helping to break up the dark matter. But every time they thought they were damaging the dark hole, it regained its power. Then, the constellations morphed out of their three-dimensional states and into billions of stars. The stars transformed into white birds and created hundreds of rings of the infinity symbol, which circled very quickly. Within a minute, the circling birds flew into the event horizon which weakened it by a thousandfold. The angels looked for the stars and prayed that they would return. As the angels went looking for the constellations, Juno, Jupiter, and Hercules continued to destroy the black hole. Slowly, over what felt like an eternity, the black hole amalgamated into a small ball. Juno caught the roundish-shaped black hole and had it spinning around on her hand. They all looked closer and could see the Milky Way inside it. It was beautiful and mesmerising.

Anxious what was occuring beyond their horizon, the angels whispered in Hercules, Jupiter, and Juno's ears. They were being warned that the rock friends were in grave danger. Instantly, they all flew as fast as the speed of light to reach their friends.

The View on the Planet of the Lilies

“What was that?!” asked Rexus. As Antares’s dark void grew three times its size and created a huge barrage of energy which reached UY Scuti, it also caused a hurricane wind to pass through the Planet of the Lilies. The trees and bushes swayed violently, and the grass that the animals stood on, caught them as the animals were forced to fall to the ground.

“Could be from the explosion of the star or the annihilation of the abyss,” replied Autumn.

“I hope it’s the black holes and they have been annihilated,” Patchy said with her teeth gritted in fear.

Figs and Tanto had been walking non-stop since the others had gone to UY Scuti. Badgers were not acclimatised to this level of worry, which was far higher than the fear of their camp not eating.

The rabbits lay on their backs and watched some shooting stars to stay calm, when suddenly they heard, "LOOK!" Figs was pointing his paws upwards. All the other animals stared up and those who were quick enough could see Hercules, Jupiter, Juno, and the four angels flying very rapidly. Four of the animals took too long to look up and by the time they did, the Roman mythological figures had disappeared into the vastness of space.

"They must be heading back to UY Scuti," shouted Harlequinn. "They first left and travelled to the west side of this planet... and I saw them not long ago travel north of here. So, they must be heading back west to get our friends… or that is what I am hoping."

"How do you know west from the east here?" asked

Tanto.

"She makes all our bridges, and any architectural work is planned by her. Harlequinn is our building planner, she made amazing maple rivers and the jungle river. Patchy also helped and co-lead the projects," replied Captain Maplelog.

"Just one maple river, Captain. It is something I have always enjoyed, building things," Harlequinn said.

"A maple river, and an Amazon River?" Good God, you rabbits are more talented than we ever gave you credit for," said Llama. "I would love to see those canals if I may?" he asked.

"Of course you can, dear Llama. Anyone from Badgercom can visit us. We will give you our sweet nectar to take home."

"Wait, something does not feel right," said Autumn.

The other animals felt it too. Their friends were in danger. The animals felt the reverberations of the destruction of the black hole. They anxiously looked up at Antares, hoping to see their friends descend and tell them that the two black voids had been obliterated. The extinction of the second black hole caused a strong gale to reach the Planet of the Lilies. People from inside their homes came out and began waving their hands up and down like an eagle spreading its wings whilst flying. They all began chanting the same song and it sounded harmonious.

THE LAST CHAPTER

The Final Hope

Saturday, early evening.

Thoric started singing a song and everyone on the rock quickly learned the lyrics and joined her:

Oh, time can tell, oh, time will tell if we shall

prevail,

Tintoretto, give me hope,

I see none through my periscope,

The red birds fade my smile,

This place is very hostile,

Oh, time can tell, oh, time will tell if we shall

prevail.

"Uh oh!" whispered Bonobo, "I knew we should not have come here," he said as he looked at Santiago and Sparrowsky.

The rock animals looked up and spotted hundreds of birds swirling a mountain to the North. These were the same red birds that had flown by just recently, but there were more now.

“The protection shield has dwindled. Oh no, what are we going to do?” shouted Laurel to the others. “What will protect us now?”

“We need to stay still and breathe lightly,” responded Cosimo. "These birds are blind but are guided by their noses, which can detect the slightest movement.”

“If we stay still, we might not be their prey,” said Thoric. But, as Thoric said this, the red birds flew dangerously close to the rock. They began flying inside different caves to look for the source of food. They had not smelled something so fresh, ever.

“No, we are in real danger,” said Sparrowsky. Sparrowsky sensed that Cosimo was worried, and he knew that the white rabbit was also losing hope.

“I am scared, Sparrowsky,” said Agent Sol.

“Me too, my friend. I have never wanted to be at Oakash camp as much I do now since we arrived in this star,” said Sparrowsky.

“Oh no, they have smelled us. They are coming towards us!!” Hopper exclaimed.

“Stand on your hind legs and get ready to attack,” Bonobos said.

The animals and humans followed Bonobos’ order and stood up on their hind legs. Their claws never looked so sharp and shiny. Even the peacocks and the crab stood upright. The peacocks opened their beautiful iridescent tails and flapped them to cool down the animals, hot from the nearby lava ‘Harrrkkkk’ they squawked. The rock started to shake as the red birds’ wings flapped nearer to them. Whoosh, the birds flew 30 feet above the rock. By now, the protective shield had all but gone. The rock friends had been spotted.

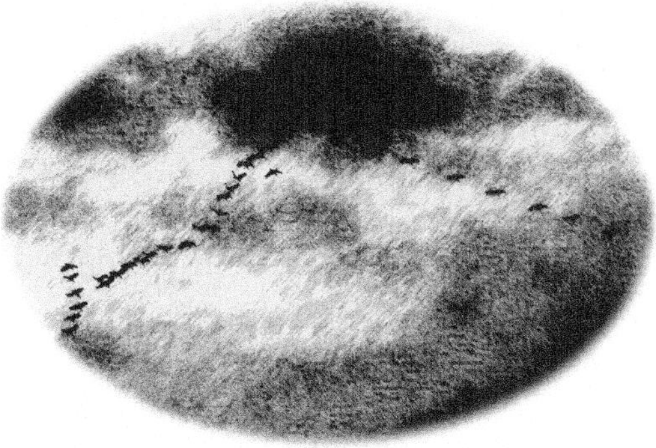

Holding tightly, everyone on the rock screamed. The death of Antares' black hole had created a second strong wind which pushed them closer to the lake.

"Arghh, hold on tightly," shouted Hopper.

"We are dangerously close to the lake now. How much more can we take of this place?" screamed John.

“They are trying to figure out what we are,” said Cosimo.

"Who is trying to work us out?" shouted Blazing Star.

“Ya, me and Cosimo strange to the hungry birds,” squawked Thoric. The crabs were pinching their claws together in fear. The peacocks were desperately fanning everyone from the mammoth heat with their strong wings.

As the hungry birds began their descent towards them and were within ten metres of being eaten, a huge, thunderous wind startled the red birds. The predators and their pack broke up. The huge wind had shocked them and pushed the rock lower down, just thirsty metres from the volcanic lava lakes.

“Arghh!!!” screamed the animals and humans.

“What was that?” asked Santiago.

“It is Hercules. Our heroes are back!” whispered Captain Lincoln with excitement. But they were not out of danger. The birds may have been discombobulated but they were quickly in their flying pack and moving towards the rock.

“It is so hot here!” screamed Little Bobbin. The heat of the magma was tremendous.

“How can we move this rock?” asked Bonobos. But before anyone could answer, they saw the birds flying towards them.

Jupiter created a V shape with his body and threw his arms and legs together. The largest streaks of lightning hit the top of the birds.

"Arkkkkk!" screamed the red birds. Several birds had been burned, whilst the others re-formed their pack and continued flying towards the rock.

The light angel held up his torch and lit the birds in his magnificent illumination. The birds were blind, so it just made them disorientated for a few seconds but they started to swirl back around in the same spot before they continued flying towards the rock. Hercules flew towards them and hit the birds with his hands and feet. One by one, the predators started to fly away or fall into the lake and die. However, many of these birds were getting away.

The net angel threw his net over nineteen birds and he caught them all. The other angel threw chains that cuffed the birds' feet. But the last thirty predators continued flying towards the rock. Juno saw the danger and flew to the rock, much faster than the birds. She stood on the rock and the animals, birds and humans instantly flocked to sit underneath her. Smack, thump, whack. Juno was defending the rock from these ravenous beasts. There were so many of them, but Juno kept moving her arms at an extraordinarily fast speed, saving the travellers from death. Jupiter put his arms in front of him and sent lightning streaks to the last fifteen. The lightning produced a strong hurricane around the flock, and Jupiter was able to hold them together and throw them thousands of miles away. Of course, the birds would be back, but the Galaxy Travellers would all be gone by then.

Hercules created a protective shield around the rock again, and the earthly beings began to cool down.

"Eat some berries!" Hercules ordered them. "It will hydrate your souls," he affirmed.

The badgers took out their berries from their bags and passed them generously to the rabbits, peacocks, the two humans and the crab who eagerly scooped them up. None of them had noticed how thirsty they had become. They were still trembling but as they began to eat the berries, the calming effects of the fruit helped them to relax. Juno and the four angels pushed the rock out of the star's atmosphere and into dark space. The animals breathed a huge sigh of relief as they left this dark star and out of the immense volcanic heat. Hercules put his arms underneath the rock and moved them towards the Planet of the Lilies.

During the return travel to the Planet of the Lilies, all the immortal and mortal souls chatted about a great many things. Jupiter realised how much he loved the earthly beings. Thoric loved the Milky Way experience Seeing the Eagle Nebula was so mesmerising for Thoric, that she did not hear Laurel speaking to her.

"Will you visit us Thoric?" she said. "Can you hear me?"

"Laurel, I go home now. But you visit me in the gallery," squawked Thoric.

"But what do you mean, visit you in a gallery?" asked Laurel.

But Thoric was too captivated by all the constellations she was seeing to answer any questions. They were passing so many constellations and old stars. With all the drama and fear when they travelled here, they had not absorbed the beauty of this galaxy as much as they did on the way back. Colours of every spectrum, bright stars and darker ones, and formations of constellations, like Hercules and Juno, began to appear out of the darkness. The angels felt happy when they saw the constellations that had pushed through the dark abyss were circling back to their positions.

"The Perseus constellation, it's moving, and so is Andromeda and..." Camila could not talk anymore. They were all speechless.

Eventually, they arrived at the atmosphere of the Planet of the Lilies and a great warmth overcame them. As they were getting lower, they could all see the people jumping up and down in joy. There were thousands of these people.

"Hooray! We are saved!" shouted the indigenous families.

The sky changed back to its normal light colours, and the animals wondered if they would lose their sense of colour on earth.

"You will see colour now, always," said Cosimo as

he read their thoughts.

All the animals snuffed their noses together in joy. The rock was placed gently on the ground by the immortal beings, and Thoric was already flying around in happiness.

In the distance, stood one of the elders, speaking to their trees to prepare them for transporting the animals and humans back to earth.

The Milky Way looked more magical and mesmerising than ever, and anyone who witnessed this evening's sky would never forget it. Hundreds of people came towards them, cheering while holding large staffs in their hands. Thump, thump; the animals could hear the vibrations of the staffs hitting the ground.

The lady who had given the badgers the crystal rock came towards them: "Thank you for saving our planet," she said. "We thank you for your kindness."

"Gosh, how can we understand you now?" asked Winstone.

“We share the same language now,” replied the wise woman.

“Thank you for the crystal rock, it took us straight into UY Scuti,” Winstone said to the women.

Autumn and Santiago embraced; she was so relieved that they, especially Santiago, had made it back safely and unharmed.

“I just wish we had a crystal rock to take us home,” murmured Llama.

“Me too, I long to see my Coco. She will love the stories that I have to tell,” said Little Bobbin.

“And so will the little un’s and all our community,” said Captain Maplelog.

“Oh yes, we’ll have many storytelling events now,” said Blazing Star.

“My brave comrades, we are going back to the painting now. We have wondered for too many years on earth,” said Cosimo. Thoric smiled and nodded her head.

“No, you cannot leave us Thoric!” said Llama and Little Bobbin at the same time.

“But you can visit us,” said Hercules as he smiled. The angels nodded too. The animals that had remained on the planet were gobsmacked. They had not met Hercules and were surprised at how friendly he was.

“It will not be the same for us, just seeing you in a painting. How will we speak to you?” asked Bonobos.

“You will be able to speak to us,” replied Cosimo.

“Our days are over on earth. We have another chance to return to our peaceful homes and sleep forever in our constellations. I have longed for this time for centuries, and thanks to earthly animals and humans, we now have reached a place of true peace. Thank you, dear Galaxy Travellers!” Hercules said.

“Yes, thank you!” said Jupiter and Juno,

The angels flew around ecstatically.

Winstone opened his backpack to put some more berries inside one of the pouches because he wanted to share them with his friends at Oakash, but he noticed there was a hole at the bottom. He dug his paws into the rip and pulled out the compass which he had found two days ago in Oakash. He saw the dials had stopped moving around rapidly. The lady asked him if she could look at it.

"This compass is working now, look, when I point it to Antares, it is north, where it should be!" she said very happily. Winstone looked at the compass and his attachment to it disappeared.

"Here, this is for you," he gave the lady his compass.

"This compass is warmly welcomed, my dear badger. I shall remember you for the rest of time," the lady said.

"LOOK!" shouted one of the children as she pointed upwards.

"Look, look, up there!" said all the children. Everyone looked up and saw two new constellations had formed near Antares. The constellations were in the shape of a badger and a rabbit.

The badgers, rabbit, Thoric and Cosimo smiled, and their hearts were filled with joy. Their quest would be forever remembered in history and tales would be told of their journey.

Everyone said their sad but warm-hearted

goodbyes, and the Galaxy Travellers and humans landed back in Ashdown Forest, Oakash on the early morning of Sunday 29th March. Hercules, the crab, peacocks, Cosimo, Juno, and Jupiter flew to planet earth from the Milky Way undetected and re-merged with their painting. It was the end of the best animal adventure, which had saved the world.

The badgers and rabbits welcomed back their friends and families and laid out huge banquets of food for the Oakash Water Diggers and Galaxy Travellers. Even Camila and John remained to join the festivities with their own families who came to join them at Oakash. The celebrations went on for thirty-two days, making the badgers the most sociable group ever for thousands of years. 'What a wonderful life we have,' thought Little Bobbin as he looked up at the Milky Way.

The National Gallery; Room 10

Monday 30th April 2020 at 8.30 am.

Gloria, an art presenter from the National Gallery walked into Room 10 to position her chair for her presentation to the school children. As Gloria entered the great room at the top of the stairs, adjacent to the large reception entrance, she dropped her books and hot drink on the floor. Her mouth opened in shock at what she was seeing. At the same time, children were waiting in the reception area downstairs, smelling lilies from the huge flowers on either side of the upstairs columns. The school children were there to hear a lecture from Gloria on 'The Origin of the Milky Way' by the artist Jacopo Tintoretto.

The children were now outside Room 10 and peering into the room at Gloria and the spillage. When she heard the children's laughter, Gloria came to. She took her glasses off and put them back on again. She walked to the feet proximity alarm but stopped short before setting it off and looked closer. She even used her glasses as if they were a microscope so she could reassure herself that she was not going mad. There was no mistaking what she saw, the eagle, which had disappeared from Tintoretto's painting four hundred and forty-five years ago, was back. And the white rabbit which had disappeared from Titian's painting was in it also. Both animal disappearances had been well documented throughout art literature history from the journals of the famous Renaissance artists, Tintoretto and Titian. Both artists had repainted the animals, but neither could get it to the standard of the original quality. Both the eagle and rabbit were exquisitely painted. Cosimo was sitting by Juno's head on the white pillow and Thoric was just above Juno's head. They were facing each other and smiling. Even Juno and Jupiter seemed happier, even though the paints on them remained the same.

"It's true, paintings bring us magic far beyond this realm," Gloria said aloud.

- THE END -

Website Resources For This Book:

https://www.animalfactsencyclopedia.com/Badger-facts.html

https://www.ashdownforest.org/wild/birds-n-beasts/mammals.php

https://www.badgertrust.org.uk/post-tradtional-badgers

https://www.coniglionatura.com/en/

https://www.forbes.com/sites/startswithabang/2018/10/26/is-anti-gravity-real-science-is-about-to-find-out/

https://www.microsoft.com/

https://www.nationalgallery.org.uk

https://nineplanets.org/questions/how-many-stars-are-in-the-milky-way/

https://nineplanets.org/uy-scuti/

https://https://www.pexels.com/

https://www.sciencefocus.com/space/harness-energy-black-hole/

https://www.sciencefocus.com/space/top-10-

largest-stars-in-the-milky-way/

https://spaceplace.nasa.gov/supernova/en/

https://www.scientificamerican.com/article/fact-or-fiction-antigravity-chambers-exist/

https://www.shutterstock.com/

Supportive Information:

Key:

Milky Way (MW)

The Rabbitdom community:

Little Bobbin (lead character) (travels to MW); (escaped from being a captive in Ottawa, Canada).

Coco Sands (Little Bobbin's wife).

Captain Marlow (Little Bobbin's best friend); (from the Orchid family and travels to MW).

Captain Stripe (also covered C.Marlow's shift, and Captain Lincoln's).

Maribel (Captain Marlow wife) (leads the strawberry field construction).

Captain Lincoln (Captain Marlow's colleague on Brown control); (travels to MW and is a fantastic leader).

Laurel Tulipa (Little Bobbin's second-best friend) (travels to MW and is good at herbal medicine).

King Roman (from an Italian rabbit colony).

Queen Reina (King Roman's wife and from England).

Twinkle (Maribel's good friend); (helps build the strawberry conservatory).

Blazing Star (King & Queen's aid for any news/vital updates and travels to MW).

Harlequinn (lead the amazon project; great at construction/planning, and travels to MW).

Rexus (Friendly and travels to MW).

Hopper (fastest rabbit and travels to MW).

Patchy (travels to MW and helped build the strawberry conservatory).

Captain Maplelog (Worked for many years, is trustworthy and travels to MW).

Luna (the cat who causes distress to the rabbits).

Mopster (silly meerkat that dug a hole for Little Bobbin).

1752 great disaster when rabbits and badgers stopped talking and being friends. It is suspected that Cosimo travelled on the travel cabins and caused mayhem, but it was necessary because he would be remembered in archive history as the oldest and wisest rabbit. Cosimo's appearance may have helped Autumn to identify him as being a necessary part of reuniting the rabbits and badgers together.

Buckshot's (male rabbits).

Buckshell's (female doe rabbits).

Rabbister- Rabbit's aged ten years or more.

Artists and associated characters:

Tintoretto (Painted the Origin of the Milky Way, 1575).

Isobel (Tintoretto's first technician).

Cristof (Tintoretto's second technician).

Titian (The Rabbit of the Madonna; the year he passes away is 1576).

Cosimo (the white rabbit) (male) (445 years old).

Thoric (eagle) (female) (445 years old).

Art painting characters:

Thoric (eagle) associated with Jupiter carrying a thunderbolt (445-year-old).

Hercules (God of strength and heroes).

Juno (Goddess of marriage & childbirth) (protector of women).

Jupiter (God of rain, lightning, and thunder) aka Zeus.

Crab.

Four angels who each carry an attribute such as a bow, net, torch and arrow, and chains.

Two peacocks, an attribute of Juno.

The badger characters:

Boars (male badgers).

Harper (co-leader for Ashdown Forest).

Oscar (co-leader for Ashdown Forest).

Bonobos (main badger character); (a MW traveller); (he's a great relative who founded Oakash).

Winstone (Bonobo's close friend); (a MW traveller); (finds a compass which he gives to an elder female in Planet of the Lilies).

Llama (elected chair speaker at the counsel meetings, and in love with Honeycot).

Sparrowsky (a MW traveller) (strong and won Olymupiad games).

Santiago (a MW traveller); (married to Autumn); (knows about the Milky way painting).

Figs (a MW traveller and is married to Floral).

Tanto (a MW traveller).

Agent Sol (a MW traveller, strong and one of the Olympiad's winner).

Trekker (the love of Venus).

Otto (from Find my Friend and replaces Thoric on Talkportation).

Treeshoot (in the rabbit welcoming line and MW traveller).

Soars-

Floral (married to Figs).

Venus (made home with Trekker).

Honeycot (Llama's love of his life).

Blossom (Autumn's best friend).

Autumn (Blossom's best friend); (married to Santiago and gets help from Thoric; and MW Traveller).

A group of badgers is called a "cette".

Olympiad's (badgers Olympics).

Badgercom is the name of the entire badger community.

Oakash is the name of the Badgercom community in Ashdown Forest.

Tule- their currency.

Location/s:

Rabbits based in Burlington, Canada, Ontario – under the Red Maple Tree.

Strawberry fields where kits are nurtured and a conservatory was built.

Rabbits aged 0-3 months are looked after by their parents in the King's Quarters groves within the Foundation Sector.

Brown Control in the Secondary Foundation.

Tertiary Foundation – closest to the exit tunnels to the great plains of the hills. The busiest of the foundations where the older rabbits work.

Orchid workers are on duty in Brown area and new bridges are found here.

Badgers are based in East Sussex, Ashdown Forest in the United Kingdom. But travel through the tunnel express to any part of the world.

Oakash and Burlington both have an Ace-Portal.

Padgercan is based in Pakistan- the cave tunnel where badgers hold yearly ceremonies and meetings.

Oakash- the Ashdown Forest badger community.

Mulberry Cave- where badgers hold their large meetings (ten rabbits, badgers, Thoric and Cosimo all attend).

Thoric knew that rabbits and badgers had never settled their differences since the disaster of 1752.

Camilla and John (in Antares and are humans from the Courtald Gallery, London).

Planet of the Lilies-

- The location within the Milky Way, where the badgers arrived from the canal tunnels.
- Tanto, Figs, Patchy, Captain Maplelog, Rexus and Harlequinn, Treeshoot and Autumn remain behind and don't travel to UY Scuti.
- Santiago, Captain Marlow, Captain Lincoln, Laurel, Blazing star, Sparrowsky, Little Bobbin, Llama, Bonobo's, Agent Sol, Winstone, Thoric, Cosimo and Hopper go to UY Scuti.

Storyline:

Occurs over one week in March, in **1575, 1576** and **2020.**

The Origin of the Milky Way (Tintoretto 1575) masterpiece is at the centre of this story.

The Madonna of the Rabbit (1530 Titian).

Two Black Holes by Antares and UY Scuti threaten to destroy everything within the Milky Way.

Cosimo and Thoric unite the rabbits and badgers

on a dangerous mission to save the galaxy from destruction.

Little Bobbin's character helps to forge new partnerships.

Thoric is a friendly bird and good friends with Cosimo.

The Talkportations miniaturise to the size of a grape during travel.

Events:

Thoric comes out of canvas on **Monday**.

Tintoretto finds that his masterpiece has been partially destroyed and is devastated by the missing image of Thoric on **Tuesday.**

Titian writes his last journal and recalls Cosimo's appearance on **Wednesday**.

The Oakash Diggers leave Oakash to dig for food on **Thursday.**

Autumn asks for Thoric's help at Find My Friend stop (10.30 am ish); Thoric travels to Ontario, leaves at 11 am and arrives in Ontario at 2 pm UK time, (in Ontario it's 7 am). Thoric then leaves Ontario at 11 am ish (takes 3 hours) and travels to Oakash (1 pm in Canada, 6 pm in England). The rabbits and badgers reunite at Oakash, and meet Cosimo on **Friday**.

The Galaxy Travellers travel through the Milky Way Portal, and alongside Hercules, Juno, Jupiter and the angels, work to obliterate the black holes on **Saturday.**

Gloria prepares to discuss the Origin of the Milky Way painting on **Sunday.**

Themes:
The colour pink occurs, which is often depicted in Renaissance paintings.
Animals- their physical characteristics e.g., agility.
Science e.g. Black holes, Scorpius, stars etc are a phenomenon.
Nature e.g. vortex's from tornadoes, trees, mud and animals etc.
Unity- mythological figures unite, as do the animals and humans.
Based over one week- Monday to Sunday activity spanned over three years in different centuries.

Printed in Great Britain
by Amazon

19191389R00149